Help! Help! I've locked myself
in the downstairs loo. Send
assistance and extra toilet
paper immediately!
M.B.

To all the stars that lit my way,
especially my parents Stefania
and Maurizio
F.S.

THE FOREST of SORROW
The Deadlands
CRACKELSER ODI
THE FAERIE HILLS
THE WILD WOODS
THE DESERT of BONES
MONSTROS CITY
N
W
E
S
SEA of DREAMS

MOUNTAINS OF THE REALLY very NORTH
DRAGON VALLEY
THE OLD COUNTRY
MOUNTAINS OF THE FAIRLY NORTH
NOWHERE
RIVER of TEARS
ISLANDS OF NIGHTMARES

A VAMPIRE CALLED KEVIN

The silent darkness of the night was split by an explosion of fire from the mouth of a galloping dragon. The magnificent creature, the colour of rubies from the Mountains of the Really Very North, thundered along a narrow rocky pass. Racing alongside her, a beautiful purple draffin – half dragon, half griffin – screeched and roared with delight. And standing on top of both, one foot on the back of each, was a nearly eleven-year-old boy.

A nearly eleven-year-old boy who was a vampire.

A vampire called Kevin.

"**WOOOOO-HOOOOOOO!**" screamed Kevin into the night, the wind in his hair and his face glowing and eyebrows singed from dragonfire. He looked behind him at the enormous train of carriages that Branwen the dragon and Gerald the draffin were pulling. The carriages belonged to Carnival Monstromo, a travelling carnival of monsters, which was Kevin's home.

Kevin and the carnival were speeding towards Monstros City to take part in the Dragon Parade at the world-famous **FESTIVAL OF FEAR**. The **FESTIVAL OF FEAR** was the most important date in the monster calendar, when carnivals from all over Grackelser Odd came together to dance, laugh, eat incredible food and watch the Dragon Parade.

This year Kevin was being allowed to ride Brannie in the parade. More than anything he wanted to help win Carnival of the Year because Carnival Monstromo had never, ever, ever, in the whole history of the **FESTIVAL OF FEAR**, won it before. Ever.

That was the reason why Kevin was out
that night: to practise something for the parade.
Something extraordinary and exciting and
dangerous. He stepped off Brannie so that both his
feet were on Gerald's back, then took a deep breath.
His plan was to jump off Gerald, then twist his body
in mid-air and perform a cartwheel, before landing
safely on Brannie's back. This move was incredibly
difficult and was known as the **DANGER DIVE
OF DEATH**.

OK, here we go. Three, two, one.

WHHHHHHHOOOOOOOOOOOOAAAAAAAA!!

Unfortunately, as he leapt, Kevin got his foot
caught in Gerald's reins. So rather than leaping
majestically, Kevin found himself dangling upside
down from the straps round Gerald's neck.

"KEVIN AURELIUS! WHAT HAVE I TOLD
YOU BEFORE ABOUT ATTEMPTING THE
DANGER DIVE OF DEATH AT THIS TIME OF
NIGHT?"

As he dangled, Kevin saw his mother standing

on top of a carriage.

"COME BACK HERE IMMEDIATELY!"

"OK, Mum," Kevin muttered through gritted fangs.

In a *puff* of smoke Kevin turned into a bat and flapped back towards the carriages, grumbling all the way. Although, to his mum, because he was a bat, it just sounded like a lot of squeaks and clicks, which was probably for the best.

CHAPTER 2

THE DRAGON PARADE

Inside the Aurelius family carriage, Kevin's best friend, Susie Cabbage, was sitting stroking Dog, who was fast asleep on her lap. Dog opened his eyes and yawned, then coughed up something green and slimy, which looked around for a moment, tutted and slithered away under the seats.

Dog was not a dog. In fact, no one was very sure what creature Dog was. Kevin's dad thought he must have some Slobbering Hounds of Hell in him on account of his enormous sharp teeth and slobber. Although that did NOT explain the wings.

Kevin the bat flapped through the open window, then fluttered around the carriage before landing gently on one of the seats. In another *puff* of smoke Kevin the boy appeared, his dark hair sticking up at strange and unusual angles and his face peppered with smudges of soot.

"What happened to you?" asked Susie.

"Oh, I was just trying out something for the Dragon Parade," he said, pulling a bag of sherbet lemons from his pocket and offering them to Susie before popping one in his mouth. "Something we should both do – me on Brannie, you on Gerald. It will be incredible."

Kevin sighed and looked at a poster next to the window. A skeleton with eyes like balls of fire was standing on the back of a golden dragon. In one hand the skeleton held a floating orb of shining white light, and in the other it held a burning flag that read: **THE FESTIVAL OF FEAR**. Underneath the picture it said: **WHO WILL WIN CARNIVAL OF THE YEAR? COME TO MONSTROS CITY TO SEE THE THRILLS! THE SPILLS! THE CHILLS!**

"I can't wait until we get to Monstros City, Susie. I'm so glad you're coming. It's the most amazing place in the whole world. You'll love it."

Susie smiled. She couldn't wait either.

"So what were you trying out for the Dragon Parade?" she asked, still smiling.

"A little move called the Danger Dive of Death," said Kevin.

"The danger dive of what?" Susie stopped smiling.

THE FESTIVAL OF FEAR

WHO WILL WIN
CARNIVAL OF THE YEAR?

Kevin looked at her. "You don't know what the Danger Dive of Death is? I thought everyone knew what the Danger Dive of Death is. I mean, it's the Danger Dive of Death."

"Well, every monster might know what it is," said Susie. "But I'm not a monster, am I?"

Susie most definitely was not a monster. Susie was a human who, until less than a week ago, had lived in a boring town where nothing interesting ever happened.

SUSIE'S PREVIOUS WEEK

MONDAY
NOTHING HAPPENED

TUESDAY
NOTHING HAPPENED

WEDNESDAY
NOTHING HAPPENED

THURSDAY
NOTHING HAPPENED

FRIDAY
NOTHING HAPPENED

SATURDAY

WENT TO A CARNIVAL, DISCOVERED THE
CARNIVAL WAS RUN BY MONSTERS!!!

SUNDAY

RODE A DRAGON FOR THE FIRST
TIME, HELPED SAVE A DRAFFIN FROM
A COLLAPSING MOUNTAIN AND
JOINED CARNIVAL MONSTROMO!!

Let's just say it had been quite a weekend.

Kevin grabbed a large book from a table next to the window; it was called **FANGS FOR THE MEMORIES: VAMPIRES FROM HISTORY**. It was one of his favourites because it was full of interesting stories about amazing vampires. He flicked through until he came to an entry about a vampire called Carmilla Le Fanu.

"Carmilla was one of the greatest performing vampires ever," he said. "She invented the Danger Dive of Death."

"It sounds quite dangerous," said Susie, before adding, "and deadly."

"Oh no," said Kevin. "It isn't dangerous because vampires are immortal. Just imagine us doing it at the Dragon Parade. We'll win Carnival of the Year for sure."

Susie tugged on the puffy sleeves of her dress. "Kevin?" she said. "The danger-deathy-dive thing sounds super, super exciting, but I'm a human, remember, so I'm not very immortal." She thought for a moment. "Actually I don't think I'm at all immortal."

But Kevin didn't hear her. He was imagining himself holding the Carnival of the Year trophy high above his head and everyone at the Festival of Fear chanting his name.

"You're right," he mumbled. "It *is* super, super exciting."

Susie frowned. Vampires might be immortal but they were not very good at listening. Not very good at all.

FANGS FOR THE MEMORIES: *Vampires from History*

Vampire: Carmilla Le Fanu

Also Known As: The Carnival Queen

Early Life: Carmilla became famous for dragon-riding and for creating the Danger Dive of Death.

Note: The Danger Dive of Death can sometimes lead to death and so should not be attempted without the correct safety goggles.

Note About the Note: Actually, the Danger Dive of Death is so dangerous that it should only be attempted by those who possess the power of immortality. Or wings. Or probably both.

CHAPTER 3

THE LEGEND OF GRAYVON FURY

Grackelser Odd rushed past the Carnival Monstromo carriage windows as they hurtled towards Monstros City. The full moon bathed the Old Country, the land of the vampires, with beautiful silvery light. Kevin could hear the night calls of the Natty Whippersnappers, jabbering and jawing in their nests, while silhouettes of Gallivanting Skew-Whiffs flittered and fluttered in the trees. Kevin gazed out of the window as enormous vampire houses rolled past.

"That's where Uncle Grando lives," he said, pointing out a particularly gigantic house in the distance. "He's the official Deputy Bringer of All Darkness. He'll probably become the actual Bringer of All Darkness in the next two or three thousand years."

Two bats flapped through the open window. They fluttered around before landing on the carriage floor and, in a *puff* of smoke, Silus and Sylvia, Kevin's older brother and sister, appeared. They were acrobats in Carnival Monstromo, and Sylvia immediately sprang up and caught hold of the curtain rail, flinging herself across the carriage and landing, perfectly, on a small reading table. Silus did a handstand, then fell into a ball and tumbled around the floor before flicking himself over Kevin's and Susie's heads and on to a luggage rack above them.

"I can't believe Mum and Dad are letting you ride in the Dragon Parade," sneered Silus. "You'll just show us all up."

"No, I won't," said Kevin.

"What were you doing outside then?" said Sylvia.

Kevin gritted his fangs and tried to ignore his sister.

"He was practising a new move for the Dragon Parade," said Susie, trying to stick up for her friend, who was the best dragon-rider she had ever seen, although admittedly, he was also the only dragon-rider she had ever seen. "The Danger Dive of Death, if you must know."

Susie immediately realised she shouldn't have said anything, as Silus and Sylvia hooted with laughter.

"More like the Rubbish Dive of Being Stupid," said Sylvia.

"You'll never be able to do that." Silus laughed, reaching over and messing up Kevin's hair.

"Get off!" yelled Kevin, then whispered to Susie, "Thanks a lot."

Sylvia glanced over at Susie as the carriage began to slow down.

"Hey, is that my acrobat outfit?" she said. "I haven't seen that in years. It looks so old."

Susie huffed. She never normally wore a dress. In fact, she didn't even own a dress. This one had been given to her by Kevin's mum, and she *hated* it. It was red and frilly and ruffly and stiff and scratchy and made Susie feel all itchy and uncomfortable. But the dress was all there was.

Four days ago, Susie had joined
Carnival Monstromo in such a
hurry that she only had one set
of clothes, which was currently
being washed.

Two more bats fluttered
through the open window before
landing on the seats opposite Kevin
and Susie. In a *puff* of smoke
Kevin's mum and dad appeared.

"Are we nearly there?"
asked Kevin.

"Not quite," said Kevin's
dad. "In fact, if we want to get
to Monstros City in time for the
Dragon Parade, we're going to
need to take a bit of a short cut."
He nodded towards the window.

Kevin and Susie looked out
and saw a large wooden sign by
the side of the road. It read:

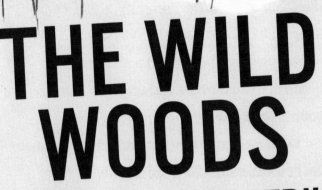

THE WILD WOODS

ENTER AT YOUR PERIL

BEWARE THE VICIOUS NITHERS

ABSOLUTELY POSITIVELY
NO PARKING BETWEEN
MIDNIGHT AND 6 A.M.

"Why are we going through the Wild Woods?" asked Sylvia.

"No one ever goes through the Wild Woods," added Silus.

Susie looked at Kevin. "Why doesn't anyone ever go through the Wild Woods?"

Silence filled every corner of the carriage like steam from a bath.

"Because," said Kevin eventually, his voice barely a whisper, "the Wild Woods is where Grayvon Fury lives."

"Oh, right, of course. Grayvon Fury," said Susie. "Er, who's Grayvon Fury?"

"Grayvon Fury is the most evil witch in the whole of Grackelser Odd," said Kevin's dad. "More evil than Erby Foulridge or Catlowe Popplewell—"

"Or Beverley Danvers," added Kevin's mum.

Twisted branches tapped and scraped against the outside of the carriage window, like bony fingers trying to claw their way inside. Kevin could see tiny wisps of blue caught in the branches that looked like faint *puffs* of smoke.

"Grayvon Fury uses the darkest of magic," said Kevin's dad. "She can transform herself into any shape she chooses—"

"Like a triangle?" interrupted Susie.

"Well, I suppose so, yes, like a triangle."

"Or a piece of toast?" asked Susie.

Kevin's dad looked at her. "I guess so," he said. "And it is said that anyone who takes anything from the woods will belong to Grayvon Fury and will have to spend the rest of their life here."

Kevin turned and looked out of the window. The trees had become so thick that the light from the moon had gone, and outside was now as dark as a yawning grave.

"Which is why it's important we get through the woods as quickly as possible," said Kevin's mum. "And that no one gets out."

No sooner had the words left her lips than the carriage shuddered and bumped and stopped dead in its tracks. For a moment, no one said anything.

Then a pair of eyes as large as dinner plates appeared outside the window. It was Gogmagog the ogre, Carnival Monstromo's Creature Keeper and driver.

"EVERYONE OK?"

"What's going on, Gog?" asked Kevin's mum.

"Is Brannie all right?" said Kevin.

"Is Gerald?" added Susie.

Gogmagog sniffed and wiped his gigantic nose with the back of his colossal hand. "THEY FINE," he said. "BUT SUMFING WRONG WIV VER BACK WHEEL."

And, with that, the enormous eyes disappeared.

Susie looked across the carriage at Kevin's mum and dad, who were staring at each other, their eyes locked with white-hot intensity. She nudged Kevin. "Are they OK?" she whispered.

"Oh, they're just talking to each other in their heads," said Kevin, stroking Dog's head. "It's something vampires can do. It's called Mind Speak."

Suddenly Susie heard something inside her head. It was a voice that seemed far away at first, then closer, like it was tuning in. And it sounded like Sylvia.

"NOT ALL VAMPIRES CAN DO IT, CAN THEY, KEVIN?"

Susie turned and looked at Sylvia, who was staring at her with a smirk on her face.

"SYLVIA, DON'T TEASE YOUR BROTHER; HE'S ONLY NEARLY ELEVEN."

Susie looked at Kevin's mum, who was also staring at her.

"AND STOP SPEAKING INSIDE SUSIE'S MIND. IT'S VERY RUDE."

Dog coughed up a splat of something orange that landed on the carpet of the carriage and then melted a hole straight through the floor.

"Right," said Kevin's dad out loud. "This is the plan. Your mum and I are going to help Gog with the wheel."

He turned to Kevin and Susie. "And we want you two to stay in here. Do NOT go outside under any circumstances."

He turned to Sylvia and Silus. "And can you two go and tell the rest of the carnival what's going on?" He paused for a moment. "Er, tell them there's nothing to worry about but they must stay in their carriages. OK?"

In four puffs of smoke Mr and Mrs Aurelius,

Silus and Sylvia turned into bats and flew out through the open window, leaving Kevin, Susie and Dog alone in the carriage.

Kevin shivered in his seat and peered into the darkness outside the window.

I HOPE WE'RE NOT LATE FOR THE DRAGON PARADE, he thought to himself.

"Pardon?" said Susie, vaguely aware of having heard someone speak. "You hope we're not what?"

Kevin turned and looked at her, surprised. "Er, I didn't say anything," he said.

FANGS FOR THE MEMORIES: *Vampires from History*

Vampire: Grando Warlock

Also Known As: The Deputy Bringer of All Darkness

History: Grando Warlock is one of the most terrifying vampires in all Grackelser Odd. He is famous for his shrieks of death-pain, and his level-ten curses. Although this almost always happens when he can't find the right kind of screwdriver or just after he has stubbed his big toe.

CHAPTER 4

LAZARUS VANDROSS

Flickering light from candles that floated in mid-air cast dancing shadows inside the Aurelius family carriage. Kevin and Susie sat in silence, listening to Gog and Kevin's mum and dad outside. The air in the carriage felt hot and Kevin slumped in his seat. Dog was sitting on Susie's lap, snoring.

Kevin thought back to what Sylvia had said in Susie's mind. It was true, one of the skills every vampire needed was the ability to Mind Speak. And it was also true that it was a skill that Kevin hadn't been able to master – yet.

Dog, he thought, trying to Mind Speak as hard as he could. *Come over to me.*

Dog opened his eyes.

Come on, Dog, thought Kevin again, concentrating with all the power of his mind. *Come to me.*

Dog looked at Kevin, then yawned, then had a scratch, then coughed up a small rock called Leslie, then closed his eyes and started snoring again.

"Are you OK?" said Susie. "You've gone a bit red."

Kevin could feel beads of sweat on his forehead from all the concentrating, and it hadn't even worked. He sighed and turned the brass handle, opening the door a crack. Cool air rushed into the carriage, bringing with it wisps of blue from the trees. Leslie the rock, who wasn't actually a rock, spotted her chance to escape, and scuttled out through the crack in the door.

"What's that smell?" asked Susie.

Kevin sniffed the air. "What smell?"

Susie took a long deep sniff. Dog's left nostril also began to quiver.

"That's funny," she said. "It's gone. I felt sure that I could smell something really delicious. Like something just out of the oven."

Dog slowly opened one eye and for just a moment his tongue popped out of his mouth and licked his lips.

Susie gave his head a playful scratch and looked at Kevin's book **FANGS FOR THE MEMORIES**. On the back cover was a picture of a vampire she recognised.

"Is that Uncle Drax?"

Kevin nodded. "Yeah, but that picture was painted about five hundred years ago."

Susie pointed at the vampire on the front cover, who was wearing a bright red suit. "Who's that?"

"Lazarus Vandross," Kevin whispered. "He's one of the most powerful vampires who has ever lived; they call him the Tormentor of Lost Souls."

Susie wasn't exactly sure what a tormentor of lost souls was, although she felt certain from looking at Lazarus Vandross that it wasn't anything good. His eyes were terrifying, almost completely black, and they seemed to stare at Susie from the cover of the book. In fact, Lazarus Vandross's picture was so hypnotic that neither Susie nor Kevin noticed Dog jump down from where he had been sleeping and pad outside.

"But you must never mention Lazarus Vandross around Uncle Drax," said Kevin. "There was a time, many centuries ago, when they were as close as brothers. But they had a huge fight three hundred and twenty-nine years ago."

Susie managed to tear her gaze away from the book. "A fight? What happened?"

Kevin looked around to make sure that no one was listening.

"No one knows exactly, but it happened on the last night of the very first **FESTIVAL OF FEAR**. They had a fight that got completely out of control and caused so much damage that there very nearly wasn't another one. Neither has spoken to the other since."

"Wow! It must've been really bad," said Susie, who felt Dog curling up by her feet.

"When did you get down?" she said, brushing threads of blue from his fur.

Another cold blast of air filled the carriage as the rest of the Aurelius family clambered back inside.

"Gog has fixed the wheel. We're heading off again," said Kevin's dad.

"YESSS!" shouted Kevin. "Dragon Parade, here we come. Let's get going!"

The carriage began to rock gently back and forth again as Gogmagog drove it forwards.

Dog let out a long low burp. Kevin looked down and saw crumbs around Dog's mouth.

That's funny, he thought. *We didn't give him anything to eat.*

FANGS FOR THE MEMORIES: Vampires from History

Vampire: Lazarus Vandross

Also Known As: The Tormentor of Lost Souls, Scourge of the Centuries, Harbinger of Fear

Fun Fact: There are no fun facts about Lazarus Vandross, only horrible ones.

CHAPTER 5

THE MISTS OF TIME

Once the Carnival Monstromo had left the
darkness of the Wild Woods, Kevin and Susie
went to sit on top of the driving carriage with Gog.

Kevin looked up at the moon. "It's four a.m.,
Gog," he said. "The Dragon Parade rehearsals
start tomorrow morning. We better hurry."

Gog made a clicking noise
and Kevin and Susie felt
the carnival carriage
lurch as Brannie
and Gerald pulled
harder and faster.
Dog, who was

sitting in Kevin's lap, lifted his head and coughed out a sad faerie (who he'd eaten a few days earlier). The faerie stood for a moment, shaking the slobber from her wings before flittering away, shouting something incredibly rude. Ignoring the insult, Dog yawned and went back to sleep.

YOU BOG-BREATHED STENCHHOLE. SOMEONE SHOULD TEACH YOU A LESSON ABOUT WHAT NOT TO EAT.

"Is Dog OK?" asked Susie, gently stroking him behind his ears.

"He's fine," said Kevin. "He coughs up things all the time. He's probably just eaten something strange."

It was true that Dog did eat a lot of strange things. In the last twenty-four hours he'd eaten seven bowls of his food, the seven bowls that the food was in, a rubbish bin full of toenail clippings, fifteen mouldy yogurts that had been at the back of the fridge for three weeks, a romantic novel about two farmers, a bucket of coal, three hairy things with nineteen legs that he'd found on the floor, two nightmares and a Caesar salad.

Susie pulled at a label that was scratching the back of her neck. Up ahead she could see pockets of yellowing fog.

"Oh no!" said Kevin, looking up at the moon again. "Not here, not now. It'd better not make us late."

"What is it?" said Susie.

"IT GET COLD NOW, HAVE THIS," Gog said, handing her a blanket. "ME HOPE WE DON'T FALL IN A BAD ONE."

Susie wrapped the blanket round her shoulders. "What's he talking about?' she whispered. "Fall into what?"

Kevin pointed at the yellow fog. "These are the Mists of Time," he said. "They pop up all over the place. Inside them are hidden timeholes."

"What does that mean?" asked Susie, pulling the blanket tight round her.

"They're holes that take you back or forward through time. Most are short, so you travel backwards or forwards just a few seconds or minutes. But some holes are bigger. They can take you back or forward years, or decades, or centuries. There are stories that some monsters have been lost in there forever, which'd better not happen today because otherwise we'll be really, really late for the Dragon Parade."

Mist wrapped itself round the carnival carriages like a damp towel and the temperature dropped. The carnival slowed down and, up ahead, Susie could see the mists begin to thin. Appearing out of the gloom was the back of another train of wooden carriages. Susie saw two people standing on the last carriage, waving at them. And not just any two people but two people who looked an awful lot like a nearly-eleven-year-old vampire and someone who was wearing a red and frilly and ruffly and stiff and scratchy dress just like hers.

"What's going on?" she asked.

"I think it's us," said Kevin. "We must be about to go through a short timehole that'll take us into the future by a few seconds."

The words had barely left his mouth when the sky suddenly went very dark.

"'OLD ON, 'ERE WE GO," said Gogmagog, as the air around them began crackling and flashing with white lightning.

Susie felt a great rush of wind and then heard a loud popping sound. The air had a tang that reminded her of a nightmare she'd once had about being chased by a gigantic evil otter called Mavis. Then the wind died and the lightning stopped.

"Come on," said Kevin, carefully putting Dog in Gog's lap before jumping up. "You'll love this."

He and Susie ran all the way down the length of the carriages until they reached the last one.

There, in the distance, they could see another train of wooden carriages pulled by Brannie and Gerald appearing out of the mist.

"There we are," said Kevin, waving his hands furiously.

Susie saw herself from a few seconds earlier looking very confused.

"Incredible," she said. "Just incredible."

CHAPTER 6

ALWAYS ANSWER "E"

For the rest of the day, and despite Gogmagog's best efforts, the Carnival Monstromo carriages fell in and out of timeholes. Most took them forward or back a few minutes, but some were deeper.

One took them so far into the future that they briefly became caught up in a battle between the Deadly Unicorns of Death (from the mountains of the Fairly North) and a race of super-evolved gigantic robot dragons. They finally reappeared from a timehole that had taken them a hundred years in the past and where Gog had accidentally married a troll princess.

"ME HAPPY ME GOT OUT OF THAT," he roared, ripping a wedding garland made of mud and crisp packets from his head.

"Well, I thought it was a lovely wedding," said Susie, holding a strange-looking sandwich. "Although I'm not sure about this. What's in it?"

"Er, cheese and anger, I think," said Kevin, sniffing it. "It's a troll speciality."

Gog pulled a beautiful shiny gold pocket watch from inside his waistcoat. He flipped open the case to look at the face of the watch. The face yawned, then blinked, and then, to Susie's great surprise, it screamed.

"IT'S FIVE IN THE MORNING! WHAT DID YOU WAKE ME UP FOR?"

Kevin smiled. "One hour," he said. "We were only in the Mists of Time for one hour."

Gog smiled and closed the pocket watch.

"GOOD," he said. "WE BACK ON TRACK."

By the time Carnival Monstromo's carriages sped across the Desert of Bones, the sun was just beginning to creep up over the horizon, bathing the skeletons that littered the golden sands in a warm orange light.

"Look," said Kevin. "There it is! There it is!"

From behind a huge dune Monstros City appeared like it was growing out of the sand. Susie could see two enormous golden towers, sticking up over the top of a pink stone wall. The wall stretched right round the city and, as they drew nearer, Susie saw just how big it was. It was so colossal that even a giant like Gogmagog would be too small to climb over. And, sitting in the middle of the gigantic wall, was a set of thick iron gates. Susie's whole body tingled with anticipation. She could hardly believe they were finally there and she was so excited that, just for a moment, she completely forgot how itchy her dress was.

The Carnival Monstromo carriages clattered to a halt in front of the enormous gates. Two bats fluttered out of the front carriage window and up to the roof. In two puffs of smoke Kevin's mum and dad appeared. On the gates was a small golden bell with a silver cord attached. Next to the bell was a sign that read **RING FOR SERVICE**. Kevin's dad grabbed the cord and yanked it hard. There was a loud ringing and a creature appeared out of thin air. A creature that looked like a giant lion with wings.

"Ah, good," said Kevin's mum.

The winged lion had the face of a woman.

"Greetings," it hissed.

Kevin's dad held up his hand. "Greetings, O mighty Sphinx, gatekeeper of Monstros City, protector of the pure, mightiest of all warriors and maker of those lovely little biscuits that you can dunk in your tea and that don't go all soggy and fall apart," he said, rolling his eyes. He bent down towards Kevin and Susie. "We have to go through this every time we come."

"Do you wish to pass?" hissed the Sphinx.

"We do, O Ancient One," Kevin's dad said. "O vision of beauty. O spectacular magnificence—"

"O get on with it," said Kevin's mum, and Susie chuckled.

"To pass through my gates," hissed the Sphinx, "you must first answer my riddle. If your answer is correct, then I shall let you pass. But if your answer is false, then I will kill you all, and also not let you in."

Susie shuffled nervously on top of the carriage roof. She did not like the sound of being killed one little bit.

The Sphinx flared her huge nostrils and snorted. "What am I? I am the beginning of everything and the end of everywhere…"

"E," said Kevin's dad.

The Sphinx carried on, regardless. "I am the beginning of eternity…"

"E!" shouted Kevin's mum.

The Sphinx didn't respond but kept on with the riddle. "I am the end of time and the end of space. What am I?"

"The letter 'E'," shouted Kevin's mum and dad and Kevin together.

The Sphinx thought for a moment, blinked, then nodded.

"Yeah, all right," it said. "In you come."

"How did you know it was 'E'?" asked Susie, as the carnival carriages started moving again.

"The answer's always 'E'," said Kevin. "It's the only riddle the Sphinx knows. She's been using it since the times of the Ancient Ones, when she used to guard the Palace of Wisdom."

"What's that?"

"It was where all the books of Grackelser Odd were kept before they invented mobile libraries."

And, with that, the Sphinx disappeared, and the huge iron gates creaked open.

MONSTROS CITY

For as long as she could remember Susie Cabbage had lived in a small quiet town in the middle of Nowhere. It was not the kind of place that had prepared her for the strangeness of seeing Monstros City.

Monsters were shouting in all directions, some selling things, some buying things, some arguing with other things. A squawking, hooting, shrieking sound vibrated through her, from the top of her head to the tips of her toes. A peculiar, unfamiliar smell hung in every street and square they passed, a bit like toasted nuts mixed with the inside of a grandma's handbag.

But the strangest thing about Monstros City was definitely the snow. Even though the sun was hot and high in the sky and there had been no sign of snow anywhere else in Grackelser Odd, the streets and rooftops glittered with a dusting of white powder and icicles sparkled from lamp posts and gutters.

"Is it always like this?" she said. "The snow, I mean?"

Kevin nodded. "Until about lunchtime," he said.

The shrieks of small monsters throwing snowballs joined hoots coming from a cluster of tables outside a café on the other side of the road. Susie could see a group of werewolves and trolls playing a game with dice. The monsters all sipped from tiny cups as they laughed and slapped the table.

As the carriages travelled deeper and deeper into Monstros City, Kevin and Susie saw that the FESTIVAL OF FEAR was in full swing. There were signs everywhere advertising music acts like GHOUL AND THE GANG, THE MOANING BONES and SUPERVAMP. Narrow streets were

crammed with stalls selling
delicious-smelling food with
funny names like Broken-teeth Pie,
Witches' Fingers and Hornsea Hodgit. Susie even
saw a small group of monsters performing street
theatre on the steps of the city hall.

It took a bit of getting used to. Everywhere
she looked, Susie could see monsters stomping,
shrieking, slithering or scuttling. She had never
seen so many different creatures in her whole life.
And while she loved the colours and the bustle and
the noise, no matter how hard she looked, Susie
couldn't see another human. Not a single one.

"Isn't this INCREDIBLE?" roared Kevin,
laughing as a skeleton strolled past, juggling
skulls.

Susie gulped and nodded. "Er, yeah,
incredible," she said, and noticed that Gerald
looked nervous too. There were dozens of dragons,
of all different colours and sizes, but no creatures
quite like Gerald.

"This is Heroes' Square," said Kevin. "This is where the parade will begin."

In the middle of the square stood an enormous statue of the three founding monsters of Monstros City: Hornsea the Dark Chimera, Ravenser the Shadow Phoenix and Dragos Aurora, the very first vampire. Susie noticed a large crack in the neck of Dragos Aurora, which looked like it had been repaired a long time ago.

"Where are the draffins?" said Susie.

"Oh, there aren't any," said Kevin, smiling. "Gerald is the only one. He's incredibly rare."

Sure enough, Susie could see that the monsters from the other carnivals were all staring and pointing at Gerald. Some were whispering, some laughing, some just standing open-mouthed as Carnival Monstromo passed by.

"How do you think that makes him feel?" asked Susie.

"Oh, I'd have thought it makes him feel very special," said Kevin in an excited whisper. "He'll be the star of the show."

Gerald looked round at Susie and she stared back into his huge deep green eyes.

"But maybe not everyone wants to be the star of the show," she said quietly.

FANGS FOR THE MEMORIES: *Vampires from History*

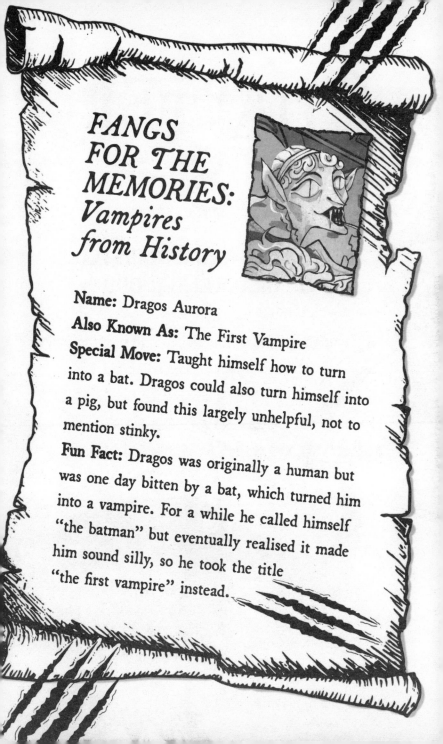

Name: Dragos Aurora

Also Known As: The First Vampire

Special Move: Taught himself how to turn into a bat. Dragos could also turn himself into a pig, but found this largely unhelpful, not to mention stinky.

Fun Fact: Dragos was originally a human but was one day bitten by a bat, which turned him into a vampire. For a while he called himself "the batman" but eventually realised it made him sound silly, so he took the title "the first vampire" instead.

CHAPTER 8

THE SEVEN GREAT CARNIVALS OF GRACKELSER ODD

Gog manoeuvred Brannie and Gerald past the other carnivals, which were all parked round the statue, like spokes on a wheel. They passed the **CARNIVAL OF BLOOD**, the **CARNIVAL OF BONES**, the **CARNIVAL OF STICKS** and the **CARNIVAL**

OF ENCHANTMENT until they reached the last remaining parking space between one carriage that had **CARNIVAL OF THE UNDEAD** written on it and another with **CARNIVAL OF THE REALLY VERY DEAD** painted on its side.

"LOOKLOOKLOOKLOOKLOOK!" Kevin gasped, grabbing Susie's shoulder. "The seven great carnivals of Grackelser Odd. All together. For the Dragon Parade."

"ATTENTION, CARNIVALS!"

Kevin stood up on top of the driving carriage and watched as a small ball of fluff wearing a huge top hat marched around the square in a very official-looking way, yelling through a large brass megaphone. "THE DRAGON PARADE REHEARSAL BEGINS TOMORROW AT DAWN! ALL CARNIVALS MUST ATTEND!"

Kevin grabbed Gog's massive arm. "Can we take Brannie and Gerald out for a practice?" he said, before adding, "Please, please, please."

Gog shook his head. **"NOPE, SORRY. VEY 'AVE BEEN TRAVELLIN' ALL NIGHT AND NEED A DRINKIE AND A RESTIE."**

As Gog stepped down from the driving carriage to untether Brannie and Gerald, other members of Carnival Monstromo appeared from their carriages and began to wander into the square. Dr Frankie Stein and Igor were the first to emerge, and immediately headed for a shop called the Emporium of Gore.

"HAVE YOU GOT THE SHOPPING LIST?" screamed Dr Frankie.

"Yes, mistress," said Igor, shuffling along, wringing his hands.

"WELL, I HOPE YOU DIDN'T FORGET TO PUT PHOENIX BEAK SLIME ON IT. I'M SICK AND TIRED OF USING YOUR SLUDGY OLD EARWAX FOR MY BRILLIANT EXPERIMENTS. IT'S RUINING THEM."

"Yes, mistress," said Igor, shoving a finger inside his ear. He wiggled it around, then pulled it out with a POP and examined the yellowy, browny, greeny, bluey earwax on the tip of his finger. Igor gave it a quick sniff, which he immediately regretted because one second later he fainted and crashed backwards into a small group of tourist skeletons.

Kevin and Susie watched as Mystic Vic, the Carnival Monstromo fortune-teller, muttered, "Doom, we're all doomed," as she wandered off towards the Demon Diner. Mystic Vic thought almost everyone was doomed nearly all the time. In the last twenty-four hours she had told Kevin, Gog, Kevin's mum and dad, Susie, Dog, a Killer Bunny and a tomato that they were all doomed. She had even told herself she was doomed yesterday morning, when she had looked at herself in the mirror.

"LOOKLOOKLOOK." Kevin nudged Susie and pointed at the Carnival of the Really Very Dead. "The ghosts are here! Look, there's Wild Oscar from Canterville," he said. "And there's the Ghost of Christmas Presents."

Kevin pointed at a ghost, who had a beautiful garland of leaves perched on top of his ghostly head.

"The ghost of Christmas presents?" repeated Susie.

"Of course!" replied Kevin, as he and Susie clambered down from the driving carriage. "Who else delivers all the presents at Christmas?"

Susie knew Kevin didn't mean to make her feel bad, but there was so much she didn't know about monsters. She went over to Gerald and gave him a big hug because she thought that he must be as nervous as she was in this strange, noisy, new place. Then she gave him a good scratch behind his ears, which made Gerald make little sighing sounds. Dog rushed over, stopped, and coughed up something purple and slimy that was wearing a large hat. The purple slimy thing looked at Susie, lifted its hat and said, "Good afternoon," before oozing away into the square.

HE'S DONE IT AGAIN, THE GHASTLY-GOBBED GHOUL!

Kevin took out his bag of sherbet lemons and gave one to Brannie and one to Gerald. Brannie snorted with delight. Sherbet lemons were her absolute favourite thing in the world. She nudged Kevin's pocket with her nose.

"No more." He laughed. "I want to show Susie around." Then he grabbed Susie's hand and dragged her towards the carriages of the Carnival of the Undead, the zombie carnival.

The first zombie Kevin and Susie met was Bonby Horkstow, who Kevin hadn't seen since the last 𝕱𝕰𝕾𝕿𝕴𝖁𝕬𝕷 𝕺𝕱 𝕱𝕰𝕬𝕽. Bonby was the zombie who looked after Gilberdyke and Goole, the dragon zombies that pulled the Carnival of the Undead along. Susie loved petting Gilberdyke and Goole, but Bonby had a rather unsettling habit of touching her head, groaning "BRAINS!", and licking his lips. So before long she whispered to Kevin that she'd like to see some of the other carnivals.

"Let's go and see the Carnival of Sticks," said Kevin.

"What sort of monsters are in that?" asked Susie, as they passed a stall that sold I-Screams.

"The Carnival of Sticks is run by witches," said Kevin.

"Witches? Like Grayvon Fury?" Susie looked at him.

Kevin smiled. "No, she's an evil witch and the Carnival of Sticks has a very strict NO EVIL WITCH policy."

They walked over to watch the witches practise their world-famous Pyramid of Spells routine. But as soon as the witches saw them, they all screamed and hurried inside, slamming the doors behind them.

Kevin shook his head. "That's weird, even for witches," he said.

In fact, only one witch said anything to them at all. Kevin and Susie said "hello" to Helen Chestnuts, at which point horror flashed across

her face, and she pointed a trembling finger at
Dog and shrieked, "THE WICKED BLUE, THE
WICKED BLUE," before running off at top speed.

CHAPTER 9

THE DANGER DIVE OF DEATH

Kevin, Susie and Dog made their way to the I-Scream stall. The heat of the afternoon sun was fierce and both Kevin and Susie needed something to cool down. Susie found it quite hard to decide exactly what flavour of I-Scream to choose because every time she selected one it shrieked at her in a most unsettling way. But eventually she plumped for a scoop of Dreadcurrant Sorbet and a scoop of Rum and Hair-raisin.

"DON'T EAT ME!" screeched the scoop of Dreadcurrant Sorbet.

"WHAT WILL BECOME OF MY CHILDREN?" cried the scoop of Rum and Hair-raisin.

Cookies and Scream
Dreadcurrant Sorbet
Rum and Hair-raisin
Shock-olate
Shock-olate Chip
Shock-olate Chip with
Shock-olate Sauce
Vanilla

Susie decided to eat their mouths first so she didn't have to listen to their cries. She looked around at the other carnivals with their beautiful painted carriages full of pictures of zombies, faeries, skeletons, vampires, witches and ghosts.

"How come all the other carnivals only have one sort of monster in them," said Susie, "but Carnival Monstromo has lots of different ones?"

"Well, the very first carnival was the Carnival of Blood, which was started by Uncle Drax, along with Lazarus Vandross and the world's funniest vampire, Count Jocular. It was so successful that the other carnivals followed soon after. And before long there were the six great carnivals of Grackelser Odd: the **CARNIVAL OF BONES**, the **CARNIVAL OF STICKS**, the **CARNIVAL OF ENCHANTMENT**, the **CARNIVAL OF THE UNDEAD** and the **CARNIVAL OF THE REALLY VERY DEAD**.

"That was why the very first **FESTIVAL OF FEAR** took place, as a way of getting all six carnivals together."

"And it's when Uncle Drax and Lazarus Vandross fell out?" checked Susie, slurping down the last of her Rum and Hair-raisin.

Kevin nodded. "After that, Uncle Drax started up his own carnival. He said he wanted it to be a place where everyone was welcome, and Carnival Monstromo was born."

Kevin took a big lick of his I-Scream.

"WAIT! NO, NO, NOOOOOOOOOOOOOO!" it screeched just as Kevin licked its mouth off.

"Apparently," he continued, "that was when Carmilla Le Fanu first performed the Danger Dive of Death too…" He stopped and looked at Susie. "Oh no! I completely forgot!" he said, grabbing Susie's hand and running back to Brannie and Gerald. "We need to practise the Danger Dive of Death."

"OH GOODY," said Gog, **"THAT HASN'T BEEN PERFORMED SINCE THERE WAS THAT AWFUL ACCIDENT, HAS IT?"**

"Wait," said Susie. "What accident?"

But Kevin had already turned into a bat and fluttered up to Brannie. Susie noticed that other members of Carnival Monstromo had started to gather by the fountain. She had only known them for a few days and was still a bit nervous around them.

"Did someone say the Danger Dive of Death'?" said Thingie, an enormous ball of blue fur.

"Er, yes," said Susie.

"OH, GOOD," said Majig, another enormous ball of blue fur. **"WE LOVE THE DANGER DIVE OF DEATH."**

"The Danger Dive of Death will spell DOOM for us all," wailed Mystic Vic, a little predictably.

Susie was starting to wish people would stop saying "Danger Dive of Death" quite so much. She watched as Kevin the bat landed on Brannie's back and turned back into Kevin the boy.

"Come on," he called, waving at her.

By now more monsters from Carnival Monstromo had stopped to see what was going on. There were Lyca, Archie and Luna Nox, the juggling werewolf family, Silus and Sylvia, Dr Frankie and Igor, and at least one Deadly Alan all staring at her.

Suddenly Susie's mouth was very dry and her palms had gone all clammy. She had ridden Gerald before and loved it. In fact, Kevin's brother and sister had said she was a natural. But this was different. She had never performed a trick before. Especially one that sounded so dangerous.

"WANT HELP?" said Gog, lifting Susie up with one hand.

"Um ... I think I'll be OK, Gog, thaaaaaaaaaaaaaaaaaaaaaaaaaaanks," said Susie, a second too late, as Gog hurled her through the air and on to Gerald's back.

"OK, I'll go first," called Kevin from Brannie's back. "Just watch what I do; it's not that hard."

"Er, OK," said Susie, grabbing the spines on Gerald's back and staggering to her feet.

She watched as Kevin took a deep breath and yelled, *"THE DANGER DIVE OF DEATH!"* before he sprang off Brannie's back. This time, everything went perfectly. Kevin twisted his body, performing an elegant mid-air cartwheel, before landing on Gerald, right behind Susie.

All the monsters cheered.

"Great job, Kevin," shouted Majig.

Kevin bowed at all the monsters. Then he turned back to Susie. "Your go," he said, his face beaming.

Susie looked across to Brannie. All she could think about was falling off.

All the monsters had quietened down again, each and every one of them watching what Susie was going to do.

"Go on then," said Kevin. "Everyone's waiting."

This is madness, thought Susie.

She looked down at her legs, which suddenly felt weak and wobbly, like they were made out of zombie jelly. "But I'm not immortal," she began, trying to explain how she felt.

"What?" said Kevin.

"I'm not immortal, like you. I don't think I can do it."

"You can, Susie. It's not too hard," said Kevin. "You just need to go for it."

Susie looked at the distance between her and Brannie. It seemed enormous. But maybe Kevin was right, maybe she just needed to go for it. She closed her eyes, took a deep breath and leapt as far as she could.

The Carnival Monstromo crowd gasped.

Everything seemed to happen both in slow motion and really, really quickly. For a moment it looked like she was going to be OK, but that moment didn't last very long. Susie thought that perhaps it had been a mistake to close her eyes just before jumping because she hadn't really looked where she was going. She soared over Brannie and landed with a splash in the fountain.

The crowd was silent, apart from Silus and Sylvia, who thought it was the funniest thing they had ever seen and roared with laughter.

Kevin jumped down and grabbed Susie's arm to pull her to her feet. Susie tried to stand up but she was so wet that she slipped and fell, landing flat on her back in the fountain again, getting even wetter. This made Silus laugh even more.

Susie sat, wet through, and looked at the other creatures from Carnival Monstromo who were staring at her in silence, no one knowing what to say.

"AT LEAST YOU NOT DEAD," said Gog, trying to say something helpful.

Susie burst into tears.

FANGS FOR THE MEMORIES: *Vampires from History*

Name: Count Jocular

Also Known As: The Monster of Mirth, the Blood-sucking Banana, the Clown Prince of Darkness

Fun Fact: Count Jocular's favourite joke: Why shouldn't you invite Lazarus Vandross to a party? Because he'll suck the life out of it.

CHAPTER 10

THE OLD VAMPIRE WAY

Back inside the Aurelius family carriage, Kevin and Susie sat and waited for Kevin's mum to find some dry clothes.

"What on earth made you want to try the Danger Dive of Death, Susie?" she said, rummaging around in a bag.

"Well," said Susie, shivering, "Kevin said—"

"I mean, if you didn't think you could do it, you really should have said something."

Susie glared at Kevin.

"I'm sure there are some clothes here that you can borrow," said Kevin's mum, looking through another bag.

"Aren't *my* clothes ready yet?" asked Susie.

"Er, not quite," said Kevin's mum. "They won't be much longer, I'm sure. There are some more clothes in a bag in the luggage carriage; I'll just pop and get them." And, with that, Kevin's mum turned herself into a bat and fluttered out of the door.

Susie snapped her head round and glowered at Kevin. "I told you I wasn't ready to do that stupid trick," she said with a scowl.

"Well, er, I…" mumbled Kevin.

"But you made me do it anyway, and I made a fool of myself in front of the whole carnival. And now your mum thinks it's my fault. There is NO WAY I'm doing that in the Dragon Parade."

Kevin was thinking about what had happened when his mum came back in holding an assortment of clothes that had obviously come from Sylvia's acrobat wardrobe.

"Here you go," she said. "Nice and dry and clean. Pick what you'd like."

Susie looked at the options. She could see
a harlequin leotard, a black-and-white tutu, a
jumpsuit made of feathers, a sparkly pair of
leggings and two capes, one silver and one bright
orange. They were all even more horrible than
the red, frilly, ruffly, stiff, scratchy dress she'd
been wearing.

"Come on, Kevin, let's give Susie some peace. I need to find your father, and you can go and check on Brannie and Gerald."

Kevin nodded and turned into a bat. He was quite relieved to flutter out of the carriage because Susie had started giving him a furious stare that was at least a ten, and probably an eleven.

After Kevin had fed and groomed Brannie and Gerald, he noticed a large crowd of excited monsters had formed next to Gog's Creature Keeper carriage. He wandered over, pushing his way through the crowd, until he could see what everyone was staring at. At the back of the Carnival Monstromo carriage train, wearing his silk pyjamas and finest black cape, flicking through an ancient dusty book and muttering to himself, was Uncle Drax.

"Uncle Drax!" he called. "What's going on? Why are you out of bed at half past two in the afternoon?"

But then Kevin heard something else, a sort of

moaning, chanting sound that seemed to be coming from all around him. The sound got louder and louder until there was a flash of lightning and a crack of thunder, and Lazarus Vandross appeared in a puff of black smoke.

Kevin stood as still as he possibly could, hoping against hope that the Tormentor of Lost Souls wouldn't notice him. Lazarus Vandross was wearing a ceremonial vampire suit cut of the finest red velvet, with a magnificent golden cloak that billowed and swished in the breeze.

But it was his eyes that were most terrifying. As Kevin stared into them, he heard the screams of a thousand curses. He shook his head, knowing that if he looked for much longer, he would be lost forever. Throughout Grackelser Odd, parents warned their children that if they didn't go to bed on time, eat up their lunch or do their homework properly, then Lazarus Vandross would find out and come for them.

Kevin fought back his terror and rushed over to his uncle and tried to pull him away. But Eli the Magnificent, a vampire from the Carnival of Blood, stopped him.

"Leave him," he growled. "Your uncle and Lazarus Vandross must settle things in the Old Vampire Way."

Kevin watched as Uncle Drax held the book up to the sky, chanting incantations, as the forces of darkness began to swirl around him like a storm. The Old Vampire Way was how vampires settled their most awful arguments. It was used only when all other ways to settle disputes had failed because the Old Vampire Way really, really hurt. A lot.

"WHAT ON EARTH IS GOING ON HERE?"

The swirling storm of the forces of darkness suddenly disappeared and every monster in the square turned to look at the Carnival Monstromo carriage train. Standing in an open doorway was Kevin's mum, looking nearly twice as cross as a Snidey Urchin.

"Honestly, Drax," she said, her hands placed firmly on her hips, "I leave you alone for thirty seconds and you try to settle things in the Old Vampire Way."

Uncle Drax stopped chanting and looked up at Kevin's mum as she climbed down from the carriage and began stalking her way towards him.

"As if I haven't got enough to do today without you doing something like this," she said.

"Er, well, i-i-it's…" began Uncle Drax, although he didn't get very far because Kevin's mum had a few more things to say.

"You're nine hundred and twelve, not one hundred and three," she said, then looked at Lazarus Vandross. "And you, Lazarus, I thought you would have known better."

The power and fury evaporated from the third-oldest vampire's eyes. "Sorry, Mrs Aurelius," he said, looking down at the ground.

"If you two want to be silly and fight in the Old Vampire Way, then you can do it after the Dragon

Parade because I'm sure we've all got a lot of work to do before then."

There was a murmur from the assembled monsters. It was true – they did have a lot to be getting on with. And, with that, Kevin's mum went back inside the carriage, slamming the door after her. Once she had gone, the sparks returned to Lazarus Vandross's eyes.

"I will abide by those terms," he said. "We shall resume after the Dragon Parade, which we will win because your scruffy carnival doesn't belong here."

Kevin felt hot and angry. "We belong here as much as you do," he muttered, as Lazarus Vandross prowled back towards the Carnival of Blood.

Maybe that's a bit how Susie feels, Kevin suddenly thought. *Like she doesn't belong here.*

He looked back at the Aurelius family carriage. Susie was sitting inside, wearing a harlequin leotard and a bright orange cape, glaring at him.

Kevin nervously smiled and waved but she didn't smile back. She just pulled the curtains across the window. Kevin's hearts sank (vampires have two, like cows, or is it squids? Well, certainly an animal with lots of legs), because even though he couldn't see her, he was certain that Susie was still glaring at him behind the curtain. She was.

FANGS FOR THE MEMORIES: *Vampires from History*

Name: Eli the Magnificent

Job: Legendary dragon-rider

Special Move: Eli's most famous move is a triple-axel-double-pleated-single-breasted front hammer. When performed correctly, this looks just like someone plummeting down to earth, only for their dragon to catch them just before they hit the ground.

Fun Fact: Before he was known as Eli the Magnificent, he went by the name Eli the Quite Good, and before that Eli the All Right, I Suppose.

CHAPTER 11

THE REHEARSAL

Susie didn't speak to Kevin for the rest of the night. She went to bed cross and then woke up cross the next morning. Dog had kept her company all night, snoring and blowing tiny wisps of blue out his mouth. Susie gave him a rub behind his ears, then adjusted her hideous leotard and peeped past the curtains out of the window.

The first fingers of sunlight were beginning to lighten the sky above Heroes' Square. Outside, Gog was giving Brannie's and Gerald's scales a polish, ready for the Dragon Parade rehearsal. Susie could also see Kevin's mum and dad, and Kevin, all standing in the shadows. They were muttering to one another and all looked very serious. Then she heard Kevin's mum say her name.

Are they talking about me? She strained to listen.

Susie heard Kevin's dad mumbling something and then saying, quite clearly, "This is a big problem. What are we going to do?"

What problem? Susie wondered. She kept listening.

"Susie's never going to fit in here," said Kevin's mum. "It's absolutely impossible."

Susie's heart started beating faster. *Is that what they think of me? That I won't fit in with the carnival?*

Finally she heard Kevin say. "Don't worry, I'll make sure she goes. I'll take her myself."

Susie felt tears prick her eyes. She felt like her heart had been broken in two. *Not you, Kevin. You want me to go too?*

She couldn't work out why they all thought she wasn't fitting in and why she would have to go. And where exactly was she supposed to go if she couldn't stay here? She'd given up everything to join Carnival Monstromo. But before she could think any more about it, the

Great Assembling Horn sounded.

"THE DRAGON PARADE REHEARSAL IS ABOUT TO BEGIN," boomed a voice across Heroes' Square.

Susie saw Kevin run off in the direction of Brannie and Gog, and Kevin's mum and dad both disappeared in puffs of smoke. Dazed, Susie stepped down from the carriage and stumbled across the square. She felt as though every monster was watching her.

Susie could see Kevin sitting on top of Brannie at the back of the parade. He tried to catch her eye but Susie didn't want to even look at him. Not after what he had said. She headed straight for Gerald, who bowed his head down so that she could climb on to his back.

"Thank you," she whispered.

Gerald snorted in the way that Susie knew meant "That's OK", so she scratched him behind his ears.

"At least you like me being here," she said, and Gerald snorted again and nuzzled her in the way that Susie knew meant "Of course I do". Then he nudged Susie on to his neck and lifted her up on to his back.

"A human?" sneered Lazarus Vandross, looking over at Susie, as he sat on an enormous silver saddle on top of the Carnival of Blood's vampire dragon. "I should have expected as much from Draximilian Aurelius's carnival. They'll take anyone in."

Susie felt anger rising inside her and she could see all the other carnivals were looking at them.

"I mean, just look at their dragons," crowed Lazarus Vandross. "They look like they haven't been groomed in years."

Susie couldn't stand it. Then suddenly every single thing that had made her feel lonely or angry over the last few days erupted out of her.

"GERALD'S NOT A DRAGON!" she roared. "HE'S A DRAFFIN! YOU SHOULD CALL HIM BY HIS PROPER NAME!"

Gerald reached his head round and nuzzled Susie.

Kevin looked over. "Susie," he said in a loud whisper, "are you OK?"

Every faerie, ghost, zombie, witch, ogre, werewolf and vampire all turned to see what Lazarus Vandross would do. No one had ever spoken to the Harbinger of Fear like that before. Well, no one had and lived. But before Lazarus Vandross had a chance to harvest Susie's soul, a voice boomed around the square.

"ATTENTION, CARNIVALS!"

Kevin looked up and saw the small ball of fluff in the top hat hovering high above the carriages, its wings extended and holding a megaphone.

"THE TIME HAS COME FOR THE DRAGON PARADE REHEARSAL. EMERGENCY EXITS TO THE SQUARE CAN BE FOUND ON THE OTHER SIDE OF THE FOUNTAIN. THE CARNIVAL OF ENCHANTMENT WILL GO ON MY FIRST WHISTLE.

GOOD LUCK, EVERYONE."

Kevin glanced up into the early-morning sky. The snow clouds looked heavy and ready to burst, and Kevin thought they looked particularly beautiful, as they seemed to be tinged with streaks of blue. He looked over at Susie. She was still boiling with anger, still not able to look in his direction. This probably meant that they weren't going to do the Danger Dive of Death any more.

There's no way we'll win Carnival of the Year now, he thought, as the whistle blew.

CHAPTER 12

THE WORST THING IN THE WORLD HAPPENS AND THEN GETS EVEN WORSE

The sun began to rise and the morning snow began to fall. The first dragons to move were the faerie dragons Ariel and Mab from the **CARNIVAL OF ENCHANTMENT**, then the ghost dragons Jessel and Quint from the **CARNIVAL OF THE REALLY VERY DEAD**, then the witchy dragons Hilda and Zelda from the **CARNIVAL OF STICKS**, then the skeleton dragons Tarsal and Talus from the **CARNIVAL OF BONES**, then the zombie dragons Gilberdyke and Goole from the **CARNIVAL OF THE UNDEAD**, then the golden vampire dragons Margo and Jerry from the **CARNIVAL OF BLOOD**, and then, right at the back, Brannie and Gerald from **CARNIVAL MONSTROMO**.

Kevin flicked his reins to get Brannie to start moving but almost immediately he could tell that something was wrong. Brannie snorted fire and turned herself right around so that she faced the Carnival Monstromo carriages, which were in completely the wrong direction to where the rest of the parade was going.

Kevin whispered to Brannie in the way that dragons from the valleys liked and knew meant "What's wrong?" But Brannie just huffed and kicked and stamped her feet.

"Get her under control," screeched Lazarus Vandross. "You're going to spook the rest of the dragons."

Gerald snarled and barged into Lazarus Vandross's vampire dragon, who started to rear and buck. It threw Lazarus Vandross off its back and sent him flying across the square.

"AAAAAAAAAHHHHHHHHHHHHHHHHHH!"

This unsettled the zombie dragons, who reared up, breathing fire in all directions. This spooked the skeleton dragons, who upset the ghost dragons, who flustered the faerie dragons. Soon jets of dragonfire swept Heroes' Square, forcing monsters to run in panic and duck for cover. The tail of Lazarus Vandross's dragon hit the head of the Dragos Aurora statue ...

which broke off and crashed into the front window
of the Emporium of Gore.

Suddenly, Brannie shot up into the air, faster than Kevin had ever felt before. He held on to her reins with all his strength as Gerald quickly followed behind.

In just a few seconds, Brannie and Gerald had flown high above the square before swooping down at top speed. Kevin clung on to Brannie's neck as tightly as he could as she landed with a thump on the roof of the Carnival Monstromo carriages, roaring her most ferocious roar.

A moment later, Gerald and Susie landed next to them.

"What's wrong with Brannie?" called Susie.

"I don't know," said Kevin, who whispered to her in the way that dragons from the valleys liked and knew meant "Please, tell me what's wrong".

Brannie craned her neck down, over the roof of the Aurelius family carriage, and looked at a patch of earth on the other side. It was the side that had been hidden from the procession. Kevin looked too and saw a patch of blue scorch marks on the ground.

"THIS IS UNACCEPTABLE!" yelled Lazarus Vandross, marching towards Carnival Monstromo, pointing a long bony finger at Brannie and Gerald. His eyes flickered with fire. "Those creatures are a menace," he snapped, spittle bubbling from his fangs. "They are uncontrollable, ill-disciplined, poorly handled, tatty-looking, unwashed and unfit to take part in the Dragon Parade. I demand

THEY'RE NOT AS MUCH OF A MENACE AS DOG!

that Carnival Monstromo be banned from the rest of the **FESTIVAL OF FEAR**."

But no one was listening to Lazarus Vandross. Everyone was looking at the blue scorches.

"What is that?" said Kevin. "It looks like something has burned the ground."

Susie jumped down from Gerald's back and looked inside the carriage. "It's here too," she said. "Inside. It's full of it."

Kevin turned himself into a bat and flapped down and turned himself back into Kevin the boy. There were scorch marks on the carriage's door and the window frames, and blue mist swirled around inside. By now some of the monsters from the other carnivals had wandered over to see what was going on.

Uncle Drax appeared in a puff of smoke. "Oh," he mumbled, the second he saw the blue scorch marks. "Oh no."

Mystic Vic shuffled up to the window of the carriage. "DOOM," she wailed for the nineteenth time since they arrived in Monstros City. "I FORSEE DOOM FOR US ALL!"

Although, judging by Helen Chestnuts's reaction, maybe Mystic Vic had a point. Kevin heard a chilling shriek and saw Helen Chestnuts's eyes goggling with fear.

"Sh-sh-she has come," she stammered, "to take what is hers."

"Who?" said Kevin.

"Gr-Gr-Grayvon Fury," said Helen Chestnuts. "The blue is the colour of her wicked magic. She has taken him."

"You're not making any sense," said Susie. "Taken who?"

But in both his hearts Kevin knew.

She had come for Dog.

And he was gone.

CHAPTER 13

VAMPIRE COUNCIL MEETING

Kevin's mind was whirling.

"Dog's gone," he said. "Grayvon Fury's got him."

Susie stood next to Kevin, not knowing what to say. She was still hurt by what she had heard earlier but she was also worried about Dog. Helen Chestnuts and the nine witches of the Carnival of Sticks began wailing and stirring a small portable bubbling cauldron.

"Did you travel here through the Wild Woods?" asked one, after they had finished wailing.

Kevin nodded. "He must have taken something from there."

"Oh, woe is he!" shrieked Helen Chestnuts. "For Grayvon Fury will have him forever."

Kevin's eyes flashed. "Then we'll fight her. We'll take Dog back like she took him."

Helen Chestnuts shook her head. "She is too powerful. She is the most evil witch who ever lived. She has set traps in those woods, traps of the strongest magic. It is said that she has created the Almost Bottomless Pit."

"Almost bottomless?" said Kevin, and Helen Chestnuts nodded. "So just a pit really," he said.

"Well, a really, really deep one," said Helen Chestnuts. "Grayvon Fury can shapeshift and can make you see things that are not there. There is no hope."

"We need an emergency vampire council meeting," said Kevin's mum. "Drax, go and get Lazarus. We need to work out the best way to get Dog back."

"I haven't asked for that vampire's help in more than three centuries," spluttered Uncle Drax.

"Then now might be a good time to start," replied Kevin's mum.

"I want to help," said Kevin.

"Me too," said Susie.

Kevin's mum smiled but shook her head. "You're both too young, I'm afraid. You must be at least two hundred years old to take part in a vampire council meeting. You need to wait for us to come up with a plan of action. There's nothing you can do."

And, with that, Uncle Drax vanished in a puff of smoke, and Kevin's mum and dad climbed into the Aurelius family carriage.

"We can't just wait for this stupid meeting," Kevin said. "They take ages to do anything. We've got to do something, Susie, right n—"

But Susie had already gone. Kevin could see her riding on Gerald's back, flying high into the sky.

"Wait for me," he said, jumping on Brannie's back and following Susie and Gerald away from Monstros City.

Back towards the Wild Woods.

Back towards Grayvon Fury.

FANGS FOR THE MEMORIES: *Vampires from History*

The Vampire Council: The vampire council is a collection of the most senior members of a vampire community. It can be formed by many different vampire covens. The vampire council can be used to sort out a variety of problems, like disputes over scourging rights, the appropriate ways to torment or organising diaries for a gala blood-tasting jamboree.

CHAPTER 14

BACK TO THE WILD WOODS

The journey from Monstros City to the Wild Woods didn't take very long. Kevin and Brannie flew at top speed across the Desert of Bones and high above the yellowing Mists of Time, trying to catch up with Susie and Gerald. But she had too much of a head start and before long Kevin saw them dive down into the dark dead trees that spread like a stain across Grackelser Odd.

As Kevin and Brannie drew closer, Kevin saw patches of Grayvon Fury's blue magic swirling below. He shivered at the thought of how frightened Dog must be. Kevin whispered in Brannie's ear in the way that dragons from the valleys liked and knew meant "Let's help Susie get Dog", and she snorted and spat fire and started her descent.

Brannie landed with a bump on the road that ran through the Wild Woods. Kevin jumped down from her back and began to look for Susie and Gerald, but there was no sign of them at all. The only tracks that Kevin could see were small and most definitely not draffin-shaped.

"I wonder what made those?" he muttered, trying his hardest not to think about Vicious Nithers. But the problem was that trying not to think about the Vicious Nithers just made Kevin think about Vicious Nithers even more. He'd read all about them and their ice-cold eyes, razor-sharp claws and row upon row of terrible teeth, and he definitely did not want to meet any.

"Susie?" he called. "Gerald? Can you hear me?"

Kevin felt like someone, or something, was watching him from the darkness of the woods. A biting wind whipped through the trees, and Kevin heard a horrible sound like distant laughter.

Up ahead the road became lost in a thicket of overgrown thorny bushes, where pale blue threads of evil magic stuck to the branches like candyfloss. To Kevin's left and right the trees were so thick they blocked out all sunlight.

"Susie?" Kevin called again. "Susie? Where are you? Can you hear me?" His words died on the cold air. "I think we should keep moving," Kevin said over his shoulder to Brannie. "We'll find them."

But when he turned to where Brannie had been standing, he saw to his horror that she was gone too. Kevin was on his own.

A horrible swell of panic began to rise inside him. He looked around again. Left, right, in front, behind. But Brannie had gone, vanished into thin air. Kevin whispered in the way that dragons from the valleys liked and knew meant "Where are you?" But there was no reply. He took out his bag of sherbet lemons, rustling them and wafting the bag around, hoping she would catch its scent, but still there was nothing.

I LOVE SHERBET LEMONS!

Kevin ran along the road towards the thicket, calling out every few paces. But as the panic-swell became a crashing panic-wave, his calls became screams.

"Susie? Brannie?"

"BRANNIE?"

"BBBRRRRAAAAAANNNNNIIIIIIIIIIIEEEEE?"

His hearts beating fast now, Kevin stumbled into the thicket, holding his arm to his face to stop the tufts of blue magic from getting in his eyes and mouth. He staggered through the bushes, flinching as thin spindly branches whipped his back. But he pushed on, moving as fast as he could, calling out Susie's and Brannie's names until his foot caught on a tree root. Kevin felt his feet suddenly stop dead in their tracks, while the rest of his body flew through the thorny branches in front him. He bounced and tumbled through the undergrowth until he found himself sprawled on his front at the edge of a small clearing.

Kevin sat up and checked for damage. His

hands and legs were scratched and his head was throbbing, but he was in one piece. The whole wood was absolutely silent and still. Kevin slowly got to his feet, knowing that he had to find his friends but not daring make a sound. There was only one thing for it. He closed his eyes and concentrated as hard as he ever had before, trying with all his might to Mind Speak.

Susie? Brannie? Dog? Are you there? Roar if you can hear me? Or shout? Or burp?

He waited for a reply. But there was nothing.

A chill wind froze Kevin to his bones and for the very first time in his life, he felt completely alone. He'd thought he'd felt alone before, but this was different. Carnival Monstromo was always busy and full of life. He never had far to go to find a friendly face, and he always knew that Gog would make him a cup of tea if he needed cheering up. But here in the Wild Woods without Susie or Brannie or Dog, he felt truly and really alone.

He thought back to all the times when Susie had

tried to explain how she felt being the only human in Monstros City and having to wear clothes she didn't like and being made to do things she didn't want to do.

It was then that Kevin heard something cut through the quiet of the wood. A slow steady chanting was coming from deep within the trees. The chanting got louder and louder until, to Kevin's horror, eight Vicious Nithers marched into the clearing. All were dressed in the traditional fighting hats of the ancient Nithers and most were carrying enormous carved Nithering sticks. Their eyes were even more icy than Kevin had imagined, their claws sharper, their teeth more terrifying. Once all eight had emerged, they stopped chanting and stared at Kevin from the other side of the clearing.

One of the Vicious Nithers stepped forwards and unfurled an enormous scroll. **"YOU HAVE ENTERED A SACRED PLACE,"** it said. **"AND FOR THIS CRIME YOU MUST BE PUNISHED."**

"I-I'm sorry," protested Kevin. "I was looking
for my friends."

A large pot appeared in a puff of smoke. In
the pot sat Brannie. She had been bound with
dragonsilk, the only material strong enough to hold
a dragon.

"Brannie!" yelled Kevin.

"THE DRAGON WILL BE COOKED IN THIS POT," said the Vicious Nither with the scroll.

"Cooked?" spluttered Kevin.

"AND BECAUSE THIS CLEARING IS OURS BY ANCIENT RITE, YOU CAN'T DO ANYTHING ABOUT IT," said the Vicious Nither. **"STAND WELL BACK BECAUSE THIS IS GOING TO GET MESSY."**

Then they formed a circle and banged their sticks together. Kevin felt something like anger, mixed with a large scoop of fear, rise up from the tips of his toes. "I'm not losing Brannie as well," he said, and without thinking he ran across the clearing towards the Vicious Nithers and Brannie in the cooking pot.

As he ran, an image of the Vicious Nithers from the pages of his favourite book, **HIDEOUS FACTS AND DISGUSTING SECRETS OF MONSTERS, BRUTES AND BEASTS**, flashed before his eyes. He had read that their feasts often lasted days, which was odd because

Vicious Nithers only ever ate salads.

Salads?

Kevin suddenly stopped running as he remembered something else. Something that Helen Chestnuts had said back in Monstros City.

She has set traps in those woods, traps of the strongest magic. Grayvon Fury can shapeshift and can make you see things that are not there.

Kevin noticed wisps of blue around the bottom of the cauldron. The wisps were the same colour as the scorch marks he'd seen in the Aurelius family carriage, after Dog had been taken.

"Wait!" shouted Kevin, pointing at the Vicious Nithers. "You are not going to eat Brannie."

The Vicious Nithers stopped banging their sticks and looked at him.

"You're vegetarians," said Kevin. "This is one of Grayvon Fury's traps."

All around him there came a shrieking sound as a strong wind whipped through the clearing. The Vicious Nithers smiled at him, baring their terrible teeth, then turned to dust, and so did the cooking pot, leaving Brannie standing in the clearing. Now Kevin could see what Grayvon Fury had been planning. Between him and Brannie lay a huge dark hole.

"**The Almost Bottomless Pit**," he murmured. "If I'd gone any further, I would have run right into it."

Kevin carefully skirted the pit because, even though it wasn't bottomless, he didn't fancy falling for a really, really long time. He released Brannie from the dragonsilk and with a great roar she reared up on her hind legs, flapping her wings. Then she picked up Kevin and tossed him on to her back.

Kevin whispered in the way that dragons from the valleys liked and knew meant "I'm so glad to see you". Then he gave her the biggest hug and a scratch behind her ears.

At the edge of the clearing, Kevin spotted more wisps of blue. He whispered again in the way that dragons from the valleys liked and knew meant "Let's go and get Susie, Gerald and Dog".

Brannie roared again and charged off at great speed, crashing through the trees and bushes, deeper and deeper into the Wild Woods.

CHAPTER 15

THE SWAMP OF LONELINESS

Kevin and Brannie soon found themselves standing on the bank of a huge steaming swamp. The water was murky and brown, and poking out of it were the shards and spikes of dead trees, their branches as sharp as blades. And there, on a small island, just out of reach of the bank, sat Gerald and Susie.

"At last we've found you," said Kevin. "Now we're back together, we need to find Dog."

Susie looked up at Kevin, her eyes puffy and red.

"Susie? Are you OK?" he said. "Have you been crying?"

Susie's bottom lip wobbled and she threw her

arms round Gerald, wailing. This made Gerald howl and shudder, tears pouring from his beautiful deep blue eyes.

Kevin whispered in the way that dragons from the valleys liked and knew meant "Is Gerald OK?" And Brannie snorted and roared at Gerald, and he huffed and snorted back. And then Brannie told Kevin that Gerald was feeling incredibly lonely because he didn't have any family.

"But we're his family," said Kevin. "He must know how much we care about him."

Brannie snorted and roared at Gerald, and he huffed back. And Brannie told Kevin that Gerald had said that he didn't know how much they cared about him because he'd only been with the carnival for a few days. And, besides, that wasn't the only thing that made him feel sad. He said that it was also because he was the only draffin at the Dragon Parade, and that, now he came to think about it, even the name Dragon Parade made him feel left out. Then Gerald cried even louder, which made

Susie sob, which set Brannie off as well.

CRACK.

The little island that Susie and Gerald were on drifted further away from the bank.

"Susie, don't cry," shouted Kevin. "We'll get you out of here."

Susie sniffed. "But I heard what you all said about me," she said. "Before the parade rehearsal. I heard what you said to your mum and dad."

"Mum and Dad? I don't know what you mean."

Susie wiped her nose on the sleeve of her harlequin leotard. "Your mum said that I'd never fit in at the carnival, and then you said I should go. None of you want me there."

CCCRRACKKK.

The island drifted further away.

"Wait, you've got it all wrong," said Kevin. "No one said you'd never fit in at the carnival. Mum was saying that you'd never fit into your *clothes*. Dad accidentally shrank them in the wash, and we knew how much you wanted them and we thought you'd be super upset."

Susie looked at him. "But I heard you say you'd show me where to go. I really thought we were best friends, Kevin."

CCCRRRAAACCCKKK.

The island moved even further away.

"We are!" shouted Kevin, as he watched Susie slowly drift into the distance. "We're best, best friends. I was saying how we should buy you some more clothes, and that I'd show you where the shop was. You know, so you could choose them."

But Susie wasn't listening – she was sobbing more than ever. Kevin thought back to how he had felt in the woods when he had been all alone. And for the very first time he understood how strange, new and scary the last few days must have been for Susie. And he realised how hurt she must have been when she had thought that no one wanted her.

CCCCRRRRAAAACCCCKKKK.

The island drifted further away. It wouldn't be long before it was completely lost from sight and then Susie and Gerald would be gone forever. Kevin looked at his friend crying and hugging Gerald and felt far away and utterly helpless. Then he noticed wisps of blue swirling around their feet.

"Susie, it's Grayvon Fury," he shouted. "This is one of her traps. The lonelier you feel, the further away you go. You're not alone, neither of you. I'm here and Brannie's here. I know we've only known each other for nearly a week but I feel like we've been friends forever. You're so brave, and you're so kind. And I'm so sorry that I didn't realise how lonely you were feeling."

Brannie snorted and roared and let Gerald know what Kevin was saying. Susie looked at Kevin.

"Susie! You've got to listen to me," shouted Kevin. "You mustn't let the sadness win. Remember that time when you tried to see how long you could wear socks on your hands before anyone noticed?"

Susie looked up. "It took ages," she said, sniffing, her voice very quiet because she was so far away. "No one noticed me."

"I know. Because they already think of you as family. Do you know how many times my mum and dad don't pay me any attention? All the time. They almost always never ask me things and before I met you no one ever listened to me at all."

Slowly Susie stopped crying and stood up, blowing her nose on her bright orange cape. And because she wasn't crying Gerald stopped too.

Kevin noticed the island had stopped moving away. "Remember when Dad was asleep," he continued, "and he farted and woke himself up, and you said—"

"Must be a squeaky floorboard," finished Susie.

"And everyone laughed, including my dad," said Kevin. "Because families can make fun of each other, and it doesn't matter."

Susie's lips half curled into a smile. "That was pretty funny," she said.

"Susie Cabbage," said Kevin, "you are not alone, and you never will be again. Both of you have a family at the carnival. For always."

And Kevin reached out and grabbed Susie because without even noticing it the island had floated all the way back to the shore because she and Gerald didn't feel lonely any more.

Susie hugged Kevin as tight as she could, and it only felt the tiniest bit weird. Brannie wrapped her wings round Gerald and nuzzled him.

"There is someone who is all alone, right now," said Susie.

Kevin nodded. "Dog!"

Somewhere in the distance they heard laughter. It was the same awful laughter that Kevin had heard in the woods.

"C'mon," he said, "let's go and get him."

CHAPTER 16

FLOOR CAKE

Kevin and Susie rode away from the Swamp of Loneliness, travelling deeper and deeper into the woods. While they rode, they saw more and more of Grayvon Fury's evil blue magic. Before long, the wisps became like tentacles, wrapping themselves round the twisted tree trunks and completely covering the floor of the wood.

Kevin shivered, unsure if it was because of how cold the wood had become, or because he was so scared.

"What's that?"

Susie was pointing at a blade of light not far ahead that cut through a thicket of trees.

Brannie and Gerald pushed through to a beautiful clearing that was flooded with warm sunlight.

"Where's all the blue gone?" asked Susie.

The blue magic that had covered the floor just moments ago had vanished. Instead a thick carpet of deep green grass stretched out in front of them, with wild flowers bursting from it like fireworks. And there, right in the middle of the grass, sat a beautiful red picnic blanket laid out with food.

"What's going on?" said Susie.

"I don't know," replied Kevin. "I really don't know."

There was no one else around, so Kevin gently tapped Brannie with his heels and they slowly walked forwards on to the grass. Gerald and Susie followed.

The picnic blanket was groaning with incredible-looking food. There were plates of enormous sandwiches, bowls of fruit, a steaming teapot, a huge chocolate cake cut into gigantic slices and a beautiful wicker picnic basket, like the kind that Susie had read about in storybooks. It had a large handle and two big flaps that covered whatever was inside.

Kevin pulled Brannie's reins and slid off her.

"What are you doing?" whispered Susie, clambering down from Gerald's back too.

"I'm just having a closer look," said Kevin, staring at the plate. "That cake looks really good."

The cake did look good. The sponge was light,

cream squidged out of the middle and it was topped by a layer of thick chocolate icing.

"Don't touch it," said Susie. "I've read enough stories to know that you should never trust unattended amazing-looking food in a wood."

"It's just delicious floor cake," said Kevin, drooling. "What's the harm in that?"

Just then, Kevin and Susie heard singing coming from behind a tree that neither of them had noticed before. A girl appeared wearing a bright blue dress, which had a big pocket at the front that was full of wild flowers. She looked about the same age as Kevin and Susie, and had long hair the colour of spun gold.

The girl smiled and began to skip over to Kevin and Susie. "Oh my, my, my," she said. "What fun to have new friends to share my picnic with. *Fiddle-de-dee*."

"Fiddle-de-dee?" whispered Susie to Kevin. "Who says 'fiddle-de-dee'?"

The girl skipped around Kevin and Susie, then skipped on to the rug and picked up the plate with the chocolate cake on. Wherever she skipped, the smell of gingerbread and puppies wafted behind her.

"Would you like to share some of my cake, Kevin?" said the girl, holding it out towards him.

The beautiful smell filled Kevin's nostrils.

I wonder how she knows my name? he thought, reaching out and grabbing a slice.

Susie wanted to tell Kevin not to eat anything but she couldn't seem to make her mouth work. And, without wanting to, her hand was reaching for the plate too and picking up a slice of cake. The girl smiled.

Kevin and Susie bit into the cake at the same time. As they did, the sunlight disappeared and the wood suddenly became as dark as night. One by one the green grass, the wild flowers, the food and picnic blanket all vanished. It had been another trap. And where the picnic basket had been, Dog now sat slumped in a swirling pool of wispy blue magic, a strange faraway look in his eyes.

Kevin wanted to run to him, to pick him up in his arms and to tell him everything was going to be all right, but he couldn't. His mouth wouldn't work and his feet were firmly planted on the ground. He had been trapped by a spell.

"I haven't told you my name, have I?" said the girl.

She clicked her fingers and wisps of blue gathered round her.

Her dress became a cloak the colour of sludge. The skin on her arms and legs and face became gnarled and knotted, like the roots of an ancient tree. And her golden hair turned brittle and white and orange, like twigs and dead branches dotted with snow.

"I'm Grayvon Fury," she rasped. "And you have just taken some cake from me, which means that you are mine forever, just like your Dog."

That was the last thing Kevin and Susie heard before they fell into a deep sleep.

CHAPTER 17

THE WORST GAME EVER!

Neither Kevin nor Susie knew how long they had been asleep, but when they woke up two things had happened.

One, they were sitting down, back to back, on the ground. Two, their arms, hands and legs were impossible to move. And, three, as hard as they tried, neither Kevin nor Susie could speak a word. OK, three things had happened while they were asleep. And Grayvon Fury had Dog in her arms and was stroking him.

No, that's four things. Let's just say lots of things had happened while they were asleep and move on. Good.

"Oh, look, my pet, they're waking up," said
Grayvon Fury, rubbing Dog's head, who was
slumped over one of her gnarled arms.

POOR DOG,
MAYBE HE'S NOT
SO BAD.

Kevin could feel Susie beginning to move
behind him. He tried to say something but couldn't.
He looked at Dog but Dog didn't look back; his
eyes seemed strange and sort of glazed over. He
was trapped in the grip of the witch's powerful
spell. On the other side of the clearing, behind a tall
tree, Kevin could see Brannie and Gerald, but they
were fast asleep.

"Oh, don't you worry about them," hissed
Grayvon Fury. "They'll be asleep for as long as
they are under my spell. I woke you two up because
now that you're mine and have to stay in the woods
forever, I thought we could play a little game. I
haven't had any friends to stay with me for, oh, let
me think, it must be nearly a thousand years. And
I'm brilliant at games."

Kevin didn't like the way Grayvon Fury said
"little game". He watched as she prowled towards
them.

"Now then," she growled, "I thought we could
play a game of hide-and-seek, which is one of my

143

favourites because I'm so good at it." The witch's eyes flashed. "But then I thought we could play hot potato, which I'm also amazing at, but then I remembered that I don't have any potatoes." Her lips curled into a crooked smile. "So then I thought we'd just play a few rounds of hang-you-upside-down-in-a-tree-while-I-throw-things-at-you, which I'm also brilliant at."

Kevin felt his legs begin to move all on their own, pulling the rest of his body towards the trunk of a tall tree. He tried to shout out but couldn't. He looked over at Susie and saw that she was moving towards the tree too, like she was being pulled by invisible rope.

I've got to do something, he thought, as he felt his body stop at the base of the tree.

He looked around the clearing again. **DOG!** he thought, trying to Mind Speak. **DOG, CAN YOU HEAR ME?**

Kevin could see Dog still slumped in Grayvon Fury's arms.

DOG! he thought as loudly as he possibly could. **DOG! YOU'VE GOT TO WAKE UP!**

But Dog didn't so much as flicker an eyelid; the magic spell was too powerful.

"Up you go!" Grayvon Fury laughed and flicked her hands.

Kevin's body heaved itself up the side of the tree, feet first. He could see Susie next to him moving in the exact same way. They went up and up and up and up. Higher and higher and higher.

"Perfect," rasped Grayvon Fury, as she put down Dog in the middle of the clearing. "This is going to be such fun."

She paused. "Well, it will be fun for me; it's going to be horrible for you two. Now, what can I throw first?"

While the witch began looking around for things to hurl at Kevin and Susie, Kevin saw that the tree they were now dangling upside down from was the tree that Brannie and Gerald were sleeping under.

BRANNIE? BRANNIE? thought Kevin,

putting all the effort he could muster into trying to Mind Speak. **BRANNIE? CAN YOU HEAR ME?**

As Kevin looked down to see if there was any reaction, the sherbert lemons that were in a bag in his pocket began to fall out and rain down to the ground, right by Brannie's head. For the briefest of moments Kevin thought he saw one of her nostrils twitch.

BRANNIE, thought Kevin again, **THERE'S A WHOLE BAG OF SHERBET LEMONS, RIGHT IN FRONT OF YOU. YOU'VE JUST GOT TO OPEN YOUR EYES.**

Brannie's nose twitched again, then her tongue flicked out, wrapped itself round one of the sweets and sucked it into her mouth.

THAT'S IT, BRANNIE, thought Kevin. **THERE ARE LOADS MORE. JUST OPEN YOUR EYES AND SEE.**

And then, just as he had asked, Brannie's left eyelid slowly opened. It blinked and looked around and saw the pile of sherbet lemons.

BRANNIE, LOOK UP. WE'RE UNDER

A MAGIC SPELL AND WE CAN'T MOVE
AND NEITHER CAN DOG. YOU'VE GOT TO
DO SOMETHING. IT'S THE WITCH.

Brannie looked up at Kevin, then she looked around and saw Grayvon Fury. Finally, in one big chomp, she ate all the sherbet lemons. The sweets gave Brannie a superpowered burst of energy and she charged across the clearing to where the witch was still wandering around looking for things to throw.

Grayvon Fury didn't know what had hit her. Whipping her tail round, Brannie catapulted the evil witch up and out of the clearing.

"AAAAAAGGGGGGHHHHHHH!"
the witch screamed, flying over the trees and landing with a crash somewhere in the woods.

As soon as she had gone, all the blue wisps in the clearing disappeared, and Grayvon's magic spell was broken. Dog immediately opened his eyes and coughed up an enormous ball of green fur. The green fur put on some tiny tap shoes, did a little dance of freedom, and flew away. Gerald woke up with a snort, just in time to catch Kevin and Susie, who had both fallen out of the tree.

Kevin jumped off Gerald and ran over to Dog, scooping him up in his arms. He was so pleased to see him that he thought about giving him a big kiss. However, Dog's fur smelled worse than the Carnival Monstromo toilet block on a hot Saturday afternoon so he didn't.

"KEVIN!" yelled Susie, sitting on top of Gerald. "LOOK OUT!"

Grayvon Fury was staggering out from the trees. She looked at Kevin holding on to Dog and shrieked with anger. Blue lightning crackled all around her, and she pointed her fingers straight at Kevin. Bolts of blue magic exploded out of her, just as Brannie flew across the clearing and grabbed Kevin and Dog in her talons. The blue lightning missed and exploded in the trees.

Grayvon Fury looked even crosser. She threw her head back and shrieked again, which was a mistake, because it gave Susie and Gerald enough time to charge straight into her and butt her back into the woods.

"LET'S GET BACK TO MONSTROS CITY," shouted Susie.

Brannie tossed Kevin and Dog on to her back and she and Gerald flew up into the sky, faster than they had ever flown before. But as Kevin glanced back over his shoulder, he saw Grayvon Fury fly out of the trees and chase right after them. This fight wasn't over yet.

CHAPTER 18

JUST DROPPING IN

Brannie and Gerald flew back towards Monstros City, high above the Desert of Bones. Far ahead, the Mists of Time swirled and formed near the banks of the Sea of Dreams. But, looking behind, Kevin saw Grayvon Fury flying on a small blue cloud, hard on their trail. He whispered to Brannie in the way that dragons from the valley liked and knew meant "Go even faster". She roared and spat fire into the sky in front of her and sped on. Gerald followed, the pair flying faster than ever before, but the witch must have cast a spell because no matter how fast they went, she kept getting closer.

Kevin looked over at Susie riding Gerald. Her head was down, her knees tucked in, in a classic riding pose. "LET'S SPLIT UP!" he shouted across to her.

Susie nodded and she and Gerald flew lower.

Kevin whispered to Brannie in the way that dragons from the valley liked and knew meant "Let's go higher". Brannie pulled her nose back and climbed up into the clouds. Behind them Kevin heard the shrieks of Grayvon Fury getting closer. Blue lightning flashed around her body and a bolt of blue magic shot from her outstretched fingers.

Quick as a flash, Kevin pushed down on Brannie's reins and she barrel-rolled down towards the Sea of Dreams. The bolt of magic flew harmlessly over their heads, exploding in the sky far above them. Grayvon Fury screamed in frustration, and the air around her crackled with blue lightning.

Kevin whispered to Brannie in the way that dragons from the valley liked and knew meant

"The witch is going to attack again". Brannie levelled off and began jagging left and right, up and down. She jerked around so much that Kevin had to hold tightly on to Dog so he wouldn't fall. Grayvon Fury kept on firing but Brannie was too quick and too clever. Bolt after bolt of blue magic fizzed past her.

But up ahead Kevin spotted a big problem. They had been jinking around so much that Susie and Gerald were now back in the witch's firing line. Kevin knew they had to change course, but before he could do anything a bolt flew past Brannie and caught Gerald's side, making him rock in the air. Susie screamed as she was thrown from Gerald's back and began tumbling down and down towards the ground.

"SUSIE!" yelled Kevin, pushing on Brannie's reins.

Brannie sped after Susie, who was spinning down towards Heroes' Square in Monstros City, her bright orange cape flapping behind her. She fell so quickly that Kevin didn't think they were going to make it. But Brannie was fast and managed to grab Susie's cape in her teeth and toss her upwards just before she hit the ground. Susie cartwheeled five times in the air, then planted her feet and landed perfectly on Brannie's back, right behind Kevin.

Kevin wanted to say something super clever, like, "so glad you could drop in". But the best he could manage was "YEEESSSSSSSSSSSSSSS" instead, which worked just as well really.

He pulled hard on Brannie's reins and she pulled her nose up just before they crashed into Heroes' Square. But the danger wasn't over.

"KEVIN!" yelled Susie.

Kevin looked behind her and saw Grayvon Fury getting closer and closer. Suddenly, a brilliant idea popped into his head and quick as a flash, he whispered his plan in Brannie's ear in the way that dragons from the valleys liked.

Brannie changed direction and Gerald followed. Kevin looked over his shoulder as evil blue magic fizzled all over Grayvon Fury's body. She pointed her arm forwards, ready to strike. And then quite suddenly, and without the slightest word of warning, Brannie, Gerald, Kevin, Susie and Dog all disappeared into thin air.

CHAPTER 19

THE "INCIDENT"

Brannie, Gerald, Kevin, Susie and Dog hadn't actually disappeared into thin air. They had disappeared into the Mists of Time. This was Kevin's plan. He wanted to try to lose Grayvon Fury deep within the yellow fog.

Brannie was flying slower now, and more carefully, just a few metres above the ground. Gerald followed. There was no telling what might be on the other side of the mists; you could be going to any place in Grackelser Odd at any point in time. The air was as hot and stale as Susie remembered.

She glanced back and saw Grayvon Fury's blue magic crackle in the fog. "She's behind us."

The mists in front of them began to clear and

Kevin and Susie saw they were flying above
Heroes' Square. It was evening, the sun was just
beginning to set, but flaming torches floated above
the square.

"Look," said Susie, pointing at a banner hanging
from the statue of Hornsea the Dark Chimera,
Ravenser the Shadow Phoenix and Dragos Aurora.

It read: **WELCOME TO THE FIRST
FESTIVAL OF FEAR.**

"We've gone back in time," said Kevin. "The
first **FESTIVAL OF FEAR** was three hundred and
twenty-nine years ago."

They swooped down into the square where a few
old-fashioned-looking carnivals had set up. One caught
Kevin's eye. It had three tatty carriages, with a sheet
hanging from the side that had **THE CARNIVAL OF
BLOOD** painted on it. Underneath were the names
VANDROSS, JOCULAR and **AURELIUS.**

Zombies, faeries, werewolves, mummies and
monsters of all shapes and sizes were staring at two
vampires near the statue.

WELCOME
TO
THE
FIRST
FESTIVAL
OF
FEAR

THE
CARNIVAL
OF BLOOD

Both were wearing black capes with enormous upturned collars. One was wearing a blue furry hat.

"It's Uncle Drax and Lazarus Vandross," said Kevin.

"HOW *DARE* YOU!" screamed Lazarus Vandross. "I'VE NEVER BEEN SO INSULTED."

"WHAT DO YOU MEAN 'INSULTED'?" yelled back Uncle Drax. "I'M ONLY TELLING THE TRUTH."

"This must be the 'incident'," said Kevin, as Brannie swooped round the statue. "I wonder why Uncle Drax is wearing that strange hat? I've never seen him wear it before, er, I mean, after."

Kevin and Susie watched as Uncle Drax roared then leapt towards Lazarus Vandross. He grabbed him by his upturned collar and threw him across the square, right through the front window of the newly opened Emporium of Gore.

"Look!" shouted Susie, as blue lightning crackled in the sky above them and Grayvon Fury appeared through the yellow mist.

"I CAN SEE YOU!" she yelled, speeding towards them.

THEY NEED TO HURRY!

"Over there," shouted Susie, pointing at a pocket of mist on the other side of the square. Brannie headed straight for it, with Gerald following close behind. And just before Grayvon Fury could catch them, the air began crackling and flashing and the Mists of Time closed round them again.

When the mists parted, Kevin and Susie saw another time reveal itself in front of them. Now they were in the Forest of Sorrow except all the trees were made of metal. A gigantic robot tree was holding a small device in its branches and was endlessly scrolling through memes posted by other robot trees all across Grackelser Odd.

"This must be the future," said Susie, as a blue bolt of lightning flashed over their heads.

Grayvon Fury emerged through the mist right behind them. She was getting closer and closer with each leap through time.

"THERE YOU ARE!" she screamed, firing blue bolts at them.

The lightning hit Gerald with full force, and he smashed into Brannie, sending all of them hurtling through the air and into another curtain of mist.

Kevin, Susie and Dog were thrown off Brannie's back, smashing into the ground. Brannie and Gerald crash-landed hard in the dirt.

Kevin staggered to his feet as Dog ran over to Susie and began licking her face. She was lying still and moaning so loudly Kevin thought she must be in great pain.

"Susie, are you OK?"

Susie looked at him. "Get Dog off me. I can taste what he had for breakfast," she said, trying hard to keep her lips closed while she spoke, and also trying hard not to think about what disgusting thing Dog might have eaten.

Kevin pulled Dog away and helped Susie up, just as Grayvon Fury flew through the mist above them and swooped down to the ground.

"Ha! Thought you could get away from me?" she screeched. "No one gets away from me because I'm the best at chasing, just like I'm the best at absolutely every game."

She's quite boastful for an evil witch, thought Kevin, as he watched the witch's body flicker all over with blue lightning.

Brannie stood up and was about to roar when Grayvon Fury fired blue magic out of her fingers at her and Gerald. Both immediately fell into a deep sleep, just like they had in the woods. Kevin checked his pockets for sherbet lemons but there weren't any left. This time they really were trapped – there was no getting away.

"Now then," said Grayvon Fury, "what are we going to do with you two—"

But then the witch stopped and looked up at something. Something that was standing behind Kevin, Susie and Dog. Grayvon Fury's blue lightning faded.

"Greetings," hissed a familiar voice.

Kevin and Susie turned round and saw an enormous winged lion with the face of a woman, standing in front of the most beautiful shimmering palace they had ever seen.

"Do you wish to pass?"

It was the Sphinx.

CHAPTER 20

TERMS & CONDITIONS

Kevin and Susie looked at the Sphinx, who was standing in front of a magnificent building that was so tall it seemed to touch the clouds.

"We must have gone back thousands of years," whispered Kevin. "The Sphinx hasn't guarded the Palace of Wisdom since the time of the Ancient Ones."

Susie looked at the palace and gasped. It was made entirely of crystals and sparkled in the sunlight. "It's beautiful."

The Sphinx regarded Grayvon Fury with a look as cold as a Jiggery-Pokery's heart.

"Do you wish to pass?" she hissed.

Grayvon Fury shook her head. "No, I do not wish to pass," she growled. "I want to take them back to the Wild Woods, where they will live with me forever. They are the rules of the game I am best at and I always win!"

Kevin looked up at the Sphinx, and then at Grayvon Fury, and an idea popped into his head.

"It's probably best that you don't want to pass," he said.

Grayvon Fury narrowed her eyes. "Why?" she rasped.

"Because only those who answer a really, really hard riddle can pass," said Kevin, winking at Susie.

The tiniest smile flickered across Susie's face. "Oh, it's probably too difficult for you," she said.

Grayvon Fury pursed her lips, then snorted. "It won't be. Because I'm amazing at riddles."

The witch turned to face the Sphinx. "Ask me your riddle," she said.

The Sphinx blinked and fixed Grayvon Fury with her stare. "Very well," she hissed. "But I will only accept your first answer to my riddle. If your answer is correct, then I shall let you pass into the Palace of Wisdom, where all the knowledge of the world is kept, and you can have access to the nice toilets on floor nine. But if your answer is wrong—"

"OH, GET ON WITH IT!" yelled the witch. "This is taking too long."

"Do you agree to my terms and conditions?" hissed the Sphinx.

"Yes, yes, yes, just hurry up," snapped Grayvon Fury.

"Very well. What am I? I am the beginning of everything and the end of everywhere. I am the beginning of eternity. I am the end of time and the end of space. What am I?"

Grayvon Fury scrunched up her nose. "Eh?" she said. "What was that first bit again?"

The Sphinx blinked. "That answer is incorrect," she said. "You have failed to answer my riddle."

"Now, hang on a minute," said Grayvon Fury, who was not used to getting something wrong. "I didn't answer. That wasn't my proper go."

"You agreed to the terms. I warned you that I would only accept your first answer and now you must pay the forfeit." The eyes of the Sphinx began to glow.

But before Grayvon Fury had a chance to say anything else, a great white bolt of lightning shot out of the eyes of the Sphinx and hit the witch in the face.

Grayvon Fury shuddered and shook for a moment, then there was a loud bang and a shower of sparks and Grayvon Fury, the most evil witch in Grackelser Odd, more wicked than Erby Foulridge or Catlowe Popplewell or Beverley Danvers, was no more. With the witch gone, her magic was gone too, and Brannie and Gerald woke from their sleep.

The Sphinx looked at Kevin. "Do you wish to pass?" she hissed.

Kevin thought about it. After all, he knew the answer to the riddle was the letter "E", but he shook his head. The idea of being able to learn all the knowledge in the world sounded like it might take most of the afternoon, and he just couldn't spare the time.

"No thanks," he said. "We really need to go."

"Yeah," said Susie. "We've got a parade to win."

Kevin smiled and he and Dog clambered on to Brannie, while Gerald lifted Susie on to his back. There was still a trail of Grayvon Fury's blue magic that they could follow back to Monstros City, so they flew quickly back through the mists.

"Oh my!" said Susie, as they travelled back past the first Festival of Fear and they saw the destruction caused by the warring vampires. Most of the buildings round the square had been destroyed, and the head of Dragos Aurora had cracked off and was sitting in the fountain getting wet.

Kevin couldn't see Uncle Drax or Lazarus Vandross anywhere. In fact, the only person in Heroes' Square was a vampire called Glenda, who was a friend of Kevin's mum. Kevin watched her picking a soaked blue furry hat out of the fountain.

Once they had gone through the last of the Mists of Time, they headed straight for Monstros City. As they flew, Kevin and Susie looked back at the Wild Woods. With Grayvon Fury's magic leaving the woods too, the darkness of the spiny, spiky trees had been replaced by a thousand shades of green. From high in the sky it looked like a glorious patchwork quilt and both Kevin and Susie thought it was the most beautiful thing they had ever seen.

CHAPTER 21

THE VAMPIRE COUNCIL'S PLAN

The sun was soft and red and beginning to set when Brannie and Gerald landed in Heroes' Square. Monsters from all the other carnivals stood silently and stared at Kevin and Susie as they made their way back to the Carnival Monstromo carriages.

The door to the Aurelius family carriage opened and out stepped Kevin's mum and dad, Uncle Drax and Lazarus Vandross, all looking very tired and very serious. The vampire council meeting that had started many hours ago, after the discovery that Dog had gone missing, was finally over.

"Good, you're here," said Kevin's dad. "We've come up with a plan."

"If we want to get Dog back, we've got to act fast," said Kevin's mum.

On hearing his name, Dog jumped down from Kevin's arms and ran straight over to Kevin's mum and began running round her legs.

Kevin's mum ignored him. "So, after much deep and careful consideration—" she continued.

Dog began sniffing her toes.

"—the vampire council has decided that it must take the following action."

Dog unfurled his wings, flapped up and began licking Kevin's mum's face.

"Wait," said Kevin's dad. "It's Dog. What's he doing here?"

"GET. HIM. OFF. ME!" yelled Kevin's mum in between licks.

Kevin pulled Dog away from his mum and put him down. Dog burped out a cloud of pink gas that floated off to find someone to haunt. "It's OK," he said. "Susie and I got him back from Grayvon Fury while you were in your meeting."

"Got him back from Grayvon Fury?" said Kevin's mum. "What? But how?"

Before Kevin or Susie could answer, all the monsters who had been silent and staring erupted into cheers and applause. The small ball of fluff who wore a large hat came over and shook Kevin's and Susie's hands.

"Incredible stuff," he said. "We all saw what happened when Grayvon Fury was chasing you."

"Kevin, that flying was amazing," said Silus.

Kevin didn't know what to say, so he just stared at his feet and went a bit red.

"And when you fell through mid-air and did those cartwheels and landed perfectly on Brannie, that was amazing," said Sylvia, smiling at Susie. "It was as good as the Danger Dive of Death."

"IT BETTER THAN THE DANGER DIVE OF DEATH," said Gog, which was something all the monsters could agree on, apart from Mystic Vic, who kept muttering about how everyone was doomed, even though they obviously weren't.

Later, after Kevin and Susie had filled in Kevin's mum and dad on exactly what had happened, Kevin's mum gave them both the biggest hug.

"I'm so glad you're both safe and sound," she said. "And I'm so proud of you both."

Susie couldn't stop smiling.

"I've got a bit of a confession to make," said Kevin's dad. "I'm really sorry, Susie, but I've shrunk your clothes. I don't think any of them are going to fit."

He held up a bundle of tiny clean clothes.

Susie narrowed her eyes. "Well, I'm never going

to fit in here, am I?"

"I'm so so sorry," said Kevin's dad, who was surprised to see Susie start to laugh.

Kevin smiled. **DON'T WORRY, DAD,** he thought. **I ALREADY TOLD SUSIE ABOUT THE CLOTHES. WE'RE GOING TO GO AND BUY SOME NEW STUFF.**

"Wait!" said Kevin's dad, his eyes sparkling and wide. "You can Mind Speak! That's incredible. Neither Silus nor Sylvia could do that when they were your age."

WELL DONE, KEVIN, mind-spoke his mum, and gave him another squeeze.

Kevin and Susie were about to head off to the Emporium of Gore to find some new clothes, when thunder clapped above their heads and rumbled around the square.

"DRAX!" yelled a voice.

Every monster's head turned and saw Lazarus Vandross, who was standing on top of a Carnival of Blood carriage, his golden cape flapping behind him.

"IT IS TIME!"

"VERY WELL," boomed Uncle Drax, who was now on top of a Carnival Monstromo carriage, his black cape fluttering in the breeze. "WE MUST SETTLE THINGS IN THE OLD VAMPIRE WAY."

"How on earth did they get up there?" said Kevin's mum.

CHAPTER 22

THE GREATEST OF DAYS

Uncle Drax stood at one side of Heroes' Square in his full ceremonial red-silk fighting pyjamas, and his hair slicked back in the way they liked in the Old Country. Across from him was Lazarus Vandross, wearing a vampire suit cut of the finest purple velvet and a necklace with a huge green stone that had once belonged to Dragos Aurora, the first vampire. Monsters of all shapes and sizes lined the square, chattering to one another and waiting for something to happen.

Eli the Magnificent, a vampire from the Carnival of Blood, stood in between Uncle Drax and Lazarus Vandross. He held up a hand and silence fell.

"We are here today to bear witness to the ending of a centuries-old feud," he began. "It will be settled in the Old Vampire Way. This is the way of things."

"This is the way of things," chanted back the watching monsters.

"The rules for this were established over a thousand years ago by the first and second vampires," continued Eli the Magnificent. "The rules have stood unaltered since then and must be followed precisely. This is the way of things."

"This is the way of things," chanted back the monsters.

"The first thing that must happen is that Draximilian Aurelius and Lazarus Vandross must state the nature of their feud."

There was silence throughout the square. No monster uttered a sound. They had waited too long to hear what had caused this legendary rift between these two ancient vampires. What was it that had soured their friendship and turned them into enemies over three hundred years ago?

"Lazarus Vandross, Scourge of the Centuries, Tormentor of Lost Souls, Harbinger of Fear," said Eli the Magnificent, "you will go first. Tell us what happened all those years ago."

Lazarus Vandross cracked his knuckles and stared at Uncle Drax. His eyes smouldered and fire crackled deep within them. "He told me my act was idiotic," he said. "It was a great insult."

The crowd of monsters gasped. This was indeed a terrible slur.

"I did not," said Uncle Drax.

The crowd of monsters gasped again.

"I said your act was 'hypnotic', not idiotic. Well, I mean, you were a hypnotist, after all."

Eli the Magnificent scratched his head with a long sharp fingernail. "So this whole feud that nearly destroyed Heroes' Square and which has lasted for over three hundred years was because of a misunderstanding?"

"Oh no," said Uncle Drax, his eyes flashing with the fire of a thousand curses. "Not at all.

Lazarus Vandross stole my blue furry hat."

The crowd of monsters gasped AGAIN. This was a most serious crime. It is widely known that you must never take a vampire's hat.

"Er, actually that was me," said a voice.

Everyone turned towards Glenda Strix, a vampire who worked in Grogg's Bottom in the Really, Really, Really Old Town. She was standing near the statue in the middle of Heroes' Square wearing a blue furry hat.

"I pulled it out of the fountain during the first **FESTIVAL OF FEAR**," she said. "I didn't know it was yours, Draximilian, I promise. Would you like it back?"

Everyone in the square looked at Uncle Drax to see what kind of terror he would rain down on Glenda Strix.

"That's OK, Glenda, you keep it," he said. "It looks great on you."

Eli the Magnificent sighed. "By the power vested in me by the monsters here present," he said, "I now declare this feud over. It is the way of things."

And all the monsters in Heroes' Square chanted, "It is the way of things."

And Uncle Drax and Lazarus Vandross shook hands and then gave one another a hug.

And then everyone cheered because even though they were quite excited to see a feud settled in the Old Vampire Way, they were also quite relieved because they knew that the Old Vampire Way always made such a lot of mess and someone would have to clear it up. And no one wanted that.

"**ATTENTION, CARNIVALS,**" boomed the voice of the small ball of fluff, who was hovering above the square. **"NOW THAT THE VAMPIRE FEUD HAS CONCLUDED WE CAN BEGIN THE DRAGON PARADE. ALL CARNIVALS TO THEIR STARTING POSITIONS."**

Kevin looked at Susie. "Come on," he said, and they rushed off to find Brannie and Gerald.

The rest of the day was the greatest of Kevin's and Susie's lives. The monster parade was better and more extraordinary and exciting than they had ever thought possible.

It began with a special fly-past from a flock of Natty Whippersnappers, whose pearly feathers changed colour as they flew overhead. First, they started off a beautiful shade of red, then turned green, before finally turning a blue so deep, they looked like the inside of a dragon egg or the first wings of a baby faerie or the juice from a freshly squeezed Yoo-hoo, only more so.

During the parade, Kevin did the Danger Dive of Death sixteen times in a row, which was a record. Susie decided not to do it because she had already done something that was even better than the Danger Dive of Death, and also because of her not being very immortal. And because she didn't have to if she didn't want to.

As they paraded around Heroes' Square, monster bands played and monster crowds cheered them on. And once the parade was over, flaming torches were lit that floated high above the square. And all the monsters danced and laughed and ate too much delicious food.

Everyone said it was the best Dragon Parade in centuries. Especially when it was announced that for their extraordinary flying and for freeing the Wild Woods from a witch more evil than Erby Foulridge, Catlowe Popplewell or Beverley Danvers, and for having the bravest dragon and draffin that anyone had ever seen, the winner of Carnival of the Year was Carnival Monstromo.

Kevin and Susie celebrated by having two Shock-olate Chip I-Screams, which they gobbled down, so they didn't have to listen to their sad pleading. And then Susie bought a new outfit to replace the one that had been ruined. She was relieved to finally put on something that wasn't an incredibly uncomfortable acrobatic costume. Susie did keep the orange cape, though, for old times' sake, and because when she wore that, it felt like absolutely anything was possible.

FLAVOURS

Cookies and Scream

Dreadcurrant Sorbet

Rum and Hair-raisin

Shock-olate

Shock-olate Chip

Shock-olate Chip with
Shock-olate Sauce

Vanilla

HAVE YOU READ?

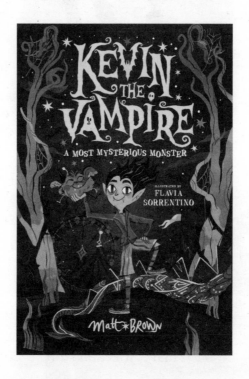

Read on for a sneak peek of
A MOST MYSTERIOUS MONSTER

ARE WE NEARLY THERE YET?

It was almost impossible to tell that Kevin Aurelius was a vampire. He looked just like any other ten-year-old.

Well, apart from his fangs obviously.

And the fact that he didn't cast a shadow.

And that he was immortal.

But apart from that it was *almost* impossible to tell.

Kevin wriggled his bottom and adjusted his shorts. His legs had become stuck to his seat, just like they always did on long journeys. He lifted them up, one at a time, and peeled them off the sticky plastic seat covering. Across from him sat his mum and dad, and over in the gloomy corner of the carriage Kevin could just make out his brother and sister, Silus and Sylvia, hanging upside down from the ceiling, whispering and giggling. They were up to something – Kevin just knew it. He sighed and glanced out of the Aurelius family carriage window, catching a glimpse of the other Carnival Monstromo carriages as they thundered round a bend on the narrow mountain pass.

Kevin felt something nuzzle his leg. He smiled and looked down as Dog sat at his feet, ears pricked, tongue lolling out of the side of his mouth.

Dog was not a dog. Nobody was very sure what he was exactly, but Kevin loved Dog with all his hearts (vampires have two, a bit like cows. Or is that stomachs? Anyway, the point is that Kevin loved Dog a lot). Kevin told all his secrets to Dog. Like the secret that he wanted to ride dragons, or the other secret that he'd once accidentally eaten someone else's earwax, or his biggest secret of all, which was that he was lonely because he didn't really have any friends. Carnival Monstromo only stopped in places long enough to put on a show, which was never enough time to meet anyone.

Kevin reached into the pocket of his shorts and pulled out a treat. Dog's tail thumped with excitement as Kevin held it up.

"Wait for it," he said, smiling. "Wait for it."

Kevin tossed the treat high into the air as Dog unfurled his furry wings and flew up. He opened his mouth wide to reveal seven razor sharp teeth, grabbing the treat in mid-air. Then, munching happily, he flew back down to settle in Kevin's lap.

"Who's a good boy then?" Kevin whispered, giving the scales on Dog's belly a scratch.

Dog looked up at Kevin, burped and coughed up a ball of fur. The ball of fur suddenly grew fifteen legs and scuttled away to the corner of the carriage.

Outside the window, the dark began to gather. Above Kevin's head, candles spluttered into life all by themselves, and cast a bright flickering light around the carriage.

LOOK OUT FOR MORE
ADVENTURES WITH

KEVIN THE VAMPIRE

COMING SOON!

ABOUT THE ILLUSTRATOR

FLAVIA SORRENTINO lives in Rome, Italy, where she grew up eating tomato sauce and colours. She loves her city and the figure of speech "Rome wasn't built in a day", which inspires her each day to seek new ways of communication and expression. If she was in the Carnival Monstromo, Flavia would be a curious cat with butterfly wings who spent their time flying and investigating strange flowers.

ABOUT THE AUTHOR

MATT BROWN has been writing
stories since a young age. His first
was in red crayon all over the living
room walls. Since then, he's written
lots of books, travelled the world
presenting TV shows and produced
radio shows and podcasts.
If he was in the Carnival Monstromo,
his act would be half dangerous,
half ridiculous and almost certainly
involve wearing a sparkly cape.

"Don't be mean to your brother," said Kevin's mum as she started to read her brochure again.

Silus and Sylvia giggled as Kevin picked up Dog and clambered out of the carriage window and up on to the roof. They knew he couldn't turn into a bat and always teased him about it. It wasn't Kevin's fault. Bat transformation was a lot harder than it looked.

a small table. "Dr Frankie and Igor are in the storage carriage. They said they needed some room for a new top-secret experiment."

"Well, you'll just have to practise on the roof," said their mum.

"The roof?" said Silus, turning towards Kevin. "Why can't *he* go on the roof?'

"Yeah, he doesn't have anything to practise." said Sylvia.

Kevin's mum looked at him. Kevin knew what was coming next. His brother and sister always got their way because they were the carnival's top performers, and Kevin wasn't good at anything yet.

"Would you mind, Kevin?" she said, smiling. "Your brother and sister need to practise and Dog would probably like a breath of fresh air."

Kevin stared at Sylvia and Silus.

"OK," he grumbled, although it wasn't OK at all.

"You can easily get up to the roof – just change into a bat and fly," sniggered Silus.

"We can't," said Sylvia. "Uncle Drax's coffin is in there."

"He's fast asleep," added Silus.

Kevin's mum raised her left eyebrow. "Hmm, that is a problem," she said.

"Yes," said Kevin's dad, stroking his pointy black beard with his long, taloned fingers. "You don't want to disturb Uncle Drax. Remember what happened the last time someone woke him up?"

Kevin's mother shuddered at the memory. The white shock at the front of her enormous beehive of black hair shivered as she did.

"It took nearly two days to clean up the mess," added Kevin's dad. "Dreadful business."

Kevin's mum turned back to Silus and Sylvia. "Can't you try the dining carriage?"

"The werewolves are in there," said Silus, performing a headstand on the arm of a chair.

"I thought the werewolves were in the storage carriage," said Kevin's dad.

"No, Dad," said Sylvia, back-handspringing off

"Someone just kicked me," he said, rubbing his head and glaring at his siblings as they leapt around the carriage, head-springing off the seats.

Kevin's mum took a deep breath. "Silus! Sylvia!" she said. "Please be more careful of your brother."

Silus tutted as he forward-rolled down the aisle. "But, Mum," he moaned.

"We're only practising," added Sylvia, backwards-rolling past Silus. "And Kevin's head always gets in the way because it's so massive."

"It is not so massive," said Kevin, a little defensively. "It's completely normal-sized for a vampire of my age."

He turned and looked at his reflection in the window (to check how big his head actually was), but then remembered vampires don't have reflections.

Kevin's mum started grinding her fangs, and a large ruby that hung from a chain round her neck began to glow, as it always did when she got angry.

"Well, go and practise in the luggage compartment," she said.

Kevin opened his book, **HIDEOUS FACTS AND DISGUSTING SECRETS OF MONSTERS, BRUTES AND BEASTS**, and began to read. He was trying to discover as much as possible about ancient sea monsters, and he'd just found a particularly interesting one. A species known as the Evil Lynns, who would lure people to the water's edge with their strange songs, then flick water right in their faces and steal their socks. Kevin was just reading about their strange underwater feeding habits (meatball spaghetti smothered in apple sauce) when a foot kicked him in the side of the head.

"OW!"

Kevin's mum looked up from the brochure she was reading. It had the words **FESTIVAL OF FEAR** on the front with a picture of a skeleton in a cape standing on the back of a fire-breathing dragon.

"Sorry, Kevin, did you say something?"